the GARFIELD show

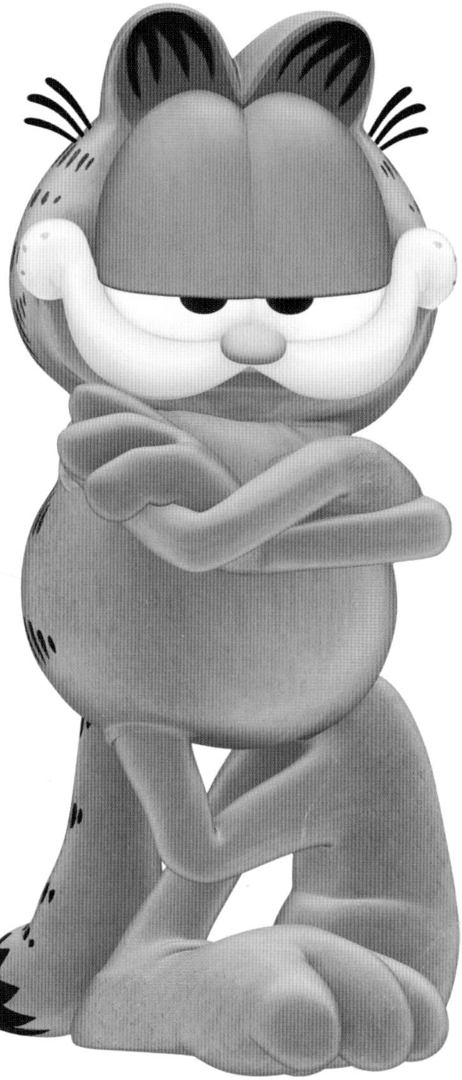

PAPERCUTZ™

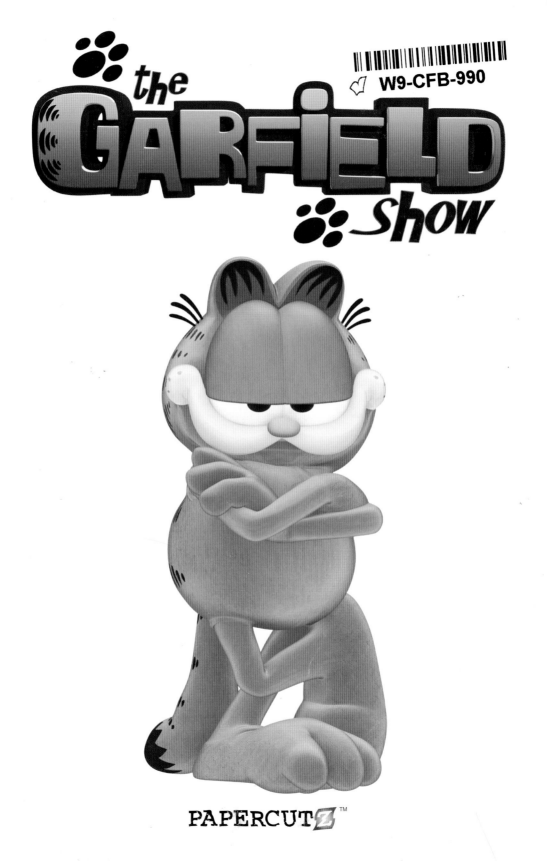

GARFIELD GRAPHIC NOVELS AVAILABLE FROM PAPERCUTZ™

GARFIELD
FISH TO FRY
& Co
PAPERCUTZ

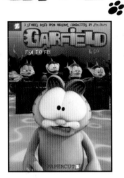

GARFIELD & Co #1
"FISH TO FRY"

GARFIELD
THE CURSE OF THE CAT PEOPLE
& CO.
PAPERCUTZ

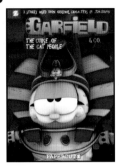

GARFIELD & Co #2
"THE CURSE OF
THE CAT PEOPLE"

GARFIELD
"CATZILLA"
& Co
PAPERCUTZ

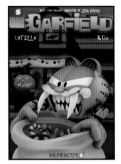

GARFIELD & Co #3
"CATZILLA"

GARFIELD
"CAROLING CAPERS"
PAPERCUTZ

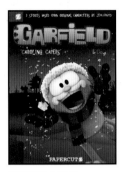

GARFIELD & Co #4
"CAROLING CAPERS"

GARFIELD
A GAME OF CAT AND MOUSE
PAPERCUTZ

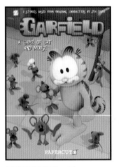

GARFIELD & Co #5
"A GAME OF CAT
AND MOUSE"

GARFIELD
MOTHER GARFIELD
& Co
PAPERCUTZ

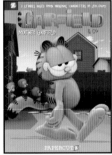

GARFIELD & Co #6
"MOTHER GARFIELD"

GARFIELD
HOME FOR THE HOLIDAYS
PAPERCUTZ

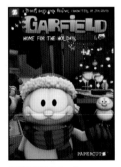

GARFIELD & Co #7
"HOME FOR THE
HOLIDAYS"

GARFIELD
SECRET AGENT X
& Co

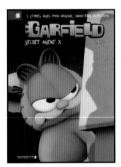

GARFIELD & Co #8
"SECRET AGENT X"

GARFIELD
show
UNFAIR WEATHER
PAPERCUTZ

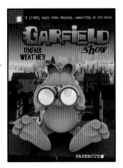

THE GARFIELD SHOW #1
"UNFAIR WEATHER"

the GARFIELD show
JON'S NIGHT OUT
PAPERCUTZ

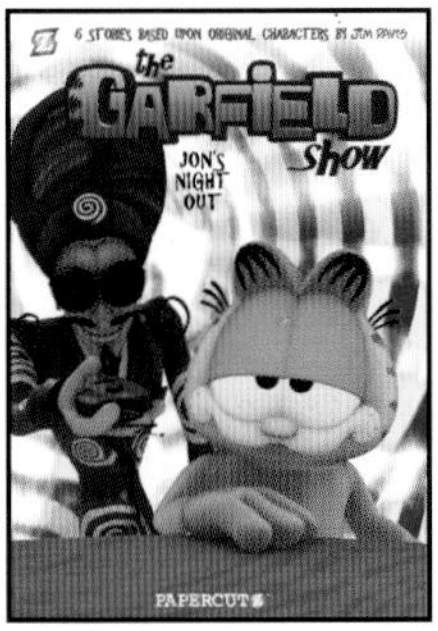

COMING SOON:
THE GARFIELD SHOW #2
"JON'S NIGHT OUT"

GARFIELD & Co GRAPHIC NOVELS ARE AVAILABLE IN HARDCOVER ONLY FOR $7.99 EACH. THE GARFIELD SHOW GRAPHIC NOVELS ARE $7.99 IN PAPERBACK, AND $11.99 IN HARDCOVER. AVAILABLE FROM BOOKSELLERS EVERYWHERE..

YOU CAN ALSO ORDER ONLINE FROM PAPERCUTZ.COM OR CALL 1-800-886-1223, MONDAY THROUGH FRIDAY, 9 - 5 EST. MC, VISA, AND AMEX ACCEPTED. TO ORDER BY MAIL, PLEASE ADD $4.00 FOR POSTAGE AND HANDLING FOR FIRST BOOK ORDERED, $1.00 FOR EACH ADDITIONAL BOOK, AND MAKE CHECK PAYABLE TO NBM PUBLISHING. SEND TO: PAPERCUTZ, 160 BROADWAY, SUITE 700, EAST WING, NEW YORK, NY 10038.

the GARFIELD show

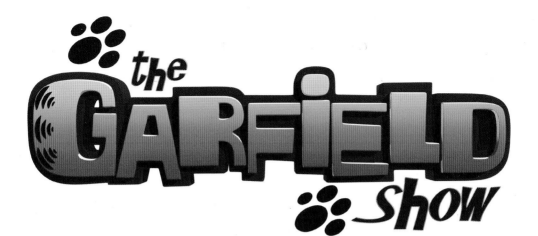

#1 "UNFAIR WEATHER"

BASED ON THE ORIGINAL CHARACTERS CREATED BY

JIM DAVIS

PAPERCUTZ™

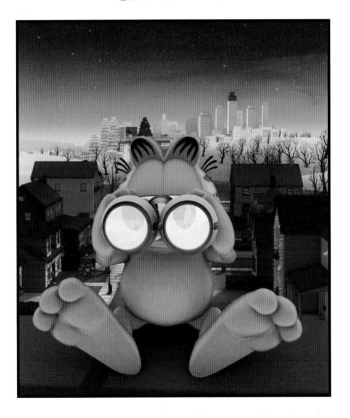

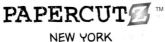

NEW YORK

THE GARFIELD SHOW #1 "UNFAIR WEATHER"

"THE GARFIELD SHOW" SERIES © 2013- DARGAUD MEDIA. ALL RIGHTS RESERVED.
© PAWS. "GARFIELD" & GARFIELD CHARACTERS ™ & © PAWS INC. - ALL RIGHTS
RESERVED. THE GARFIELD SHOW—A DARGAUD MEDIA PRODUCTION. IN ASSO-
CIATION WITH FRANCE3 WITH THE PARTICIPATION OF CENTRE NATIONAL DE LA
CINÉMETOGRAPHIE AND THE SUPPORT OF REGION ILE-DE-FRANCE. A SERIES DE-
VELOPED BY PHILIPPE VIDAL, ROBERT REA AND STEVE BALISSAT. BASED UPON
THE CHARACTERS CREATED BY JIM DAVIS. ORIGINAL STORIES: "UNFAIR WEATH-
ER" AND "WICKED WISHES" WRITTEN BY MARK EVANIER; "MAILMAN BLUES" WRIT-
TEN BY PETER BERTS; "THE ROBOT" WRITTEN BY BAPTISTE HEIDRICH; "DOWN ON
THE FARM" WRITTEN BY CHRISTOPHE POUJOL.

CEDRIC MICHIELS - COMICS ADAPTATION
JOE JOHNSON - TRANSLATIONS
JIM SALICRUP - DIALOGUE RESTORATION
JANICE CHIANG - LETTERING
BETH SCORZATO - PRODUCTION COORDINATOR
MICHAEL PETRANEK - EDITOR
JIM SALICRUP
EDITOR-IN-CHIEF

ISBN: 978-1-59707-422-3 PAPERBACK EDITION
ISBN: 978-1-59707-433-9 HARDCOVER EDITION

PRINTED IN CHINA
MAY 2013 BY O.G. PRINTING PRODUCTIONS, LTD.
UNITS 2 & 3, 5/F, LEMMI CENTRE
50 HOI YUEN ROAD
KWON TONG, KOWLOON

PAPERCUTZ BOOKS MAY BE PURCHASED FOR BUSINESS OR PROMOTIONAL USE. FOR INFORMATION ON
BULK PURCHASES PLEASE CONTACT MACMILLAN CORPORATE AND PREMIUM SALES DEPARTMENT AT
(800) 221-7945 X5442.

DISTRIBUTED BY MACMILLAN

FIRST PAPERCUTZ PRINTING

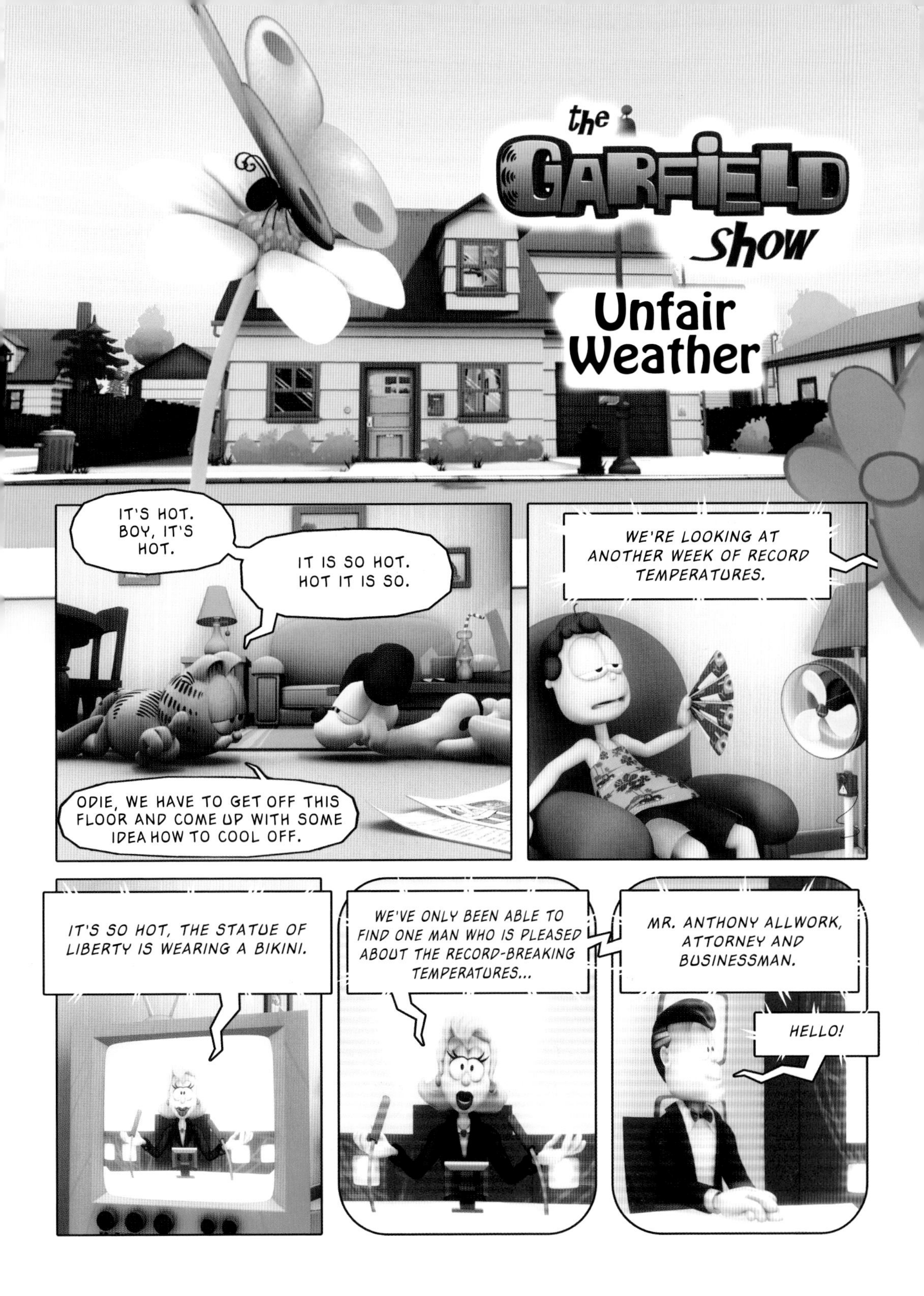
the GARFIELD show
Unfair Weather
IT'S HOT. BOY, IT'S HOT.
IT IS SO HOT. HOT IT IS SO.
ODIE, WE HAVE TO GET OFF THIS FLOOR AND COME UP WITH SOME IDEA HOW TO COOL OFF.
WE'RE LOOKING AT ANOTHER WEEK OF RECORD TEMPERATURES.
IT'S SO HOT, THE STATUE OF LIBERTY IS WEARING A BIKINI.
WE'VE ONLY BEEN ABLE TO FIND ONE MAN WHO IS PLEASED ABOUT THE RECORD-BREAKING TEMPERATURES...
MR. ANTHONY ALLWORK, ATTORNEY AND BUSINESSMAN.
HELLO!

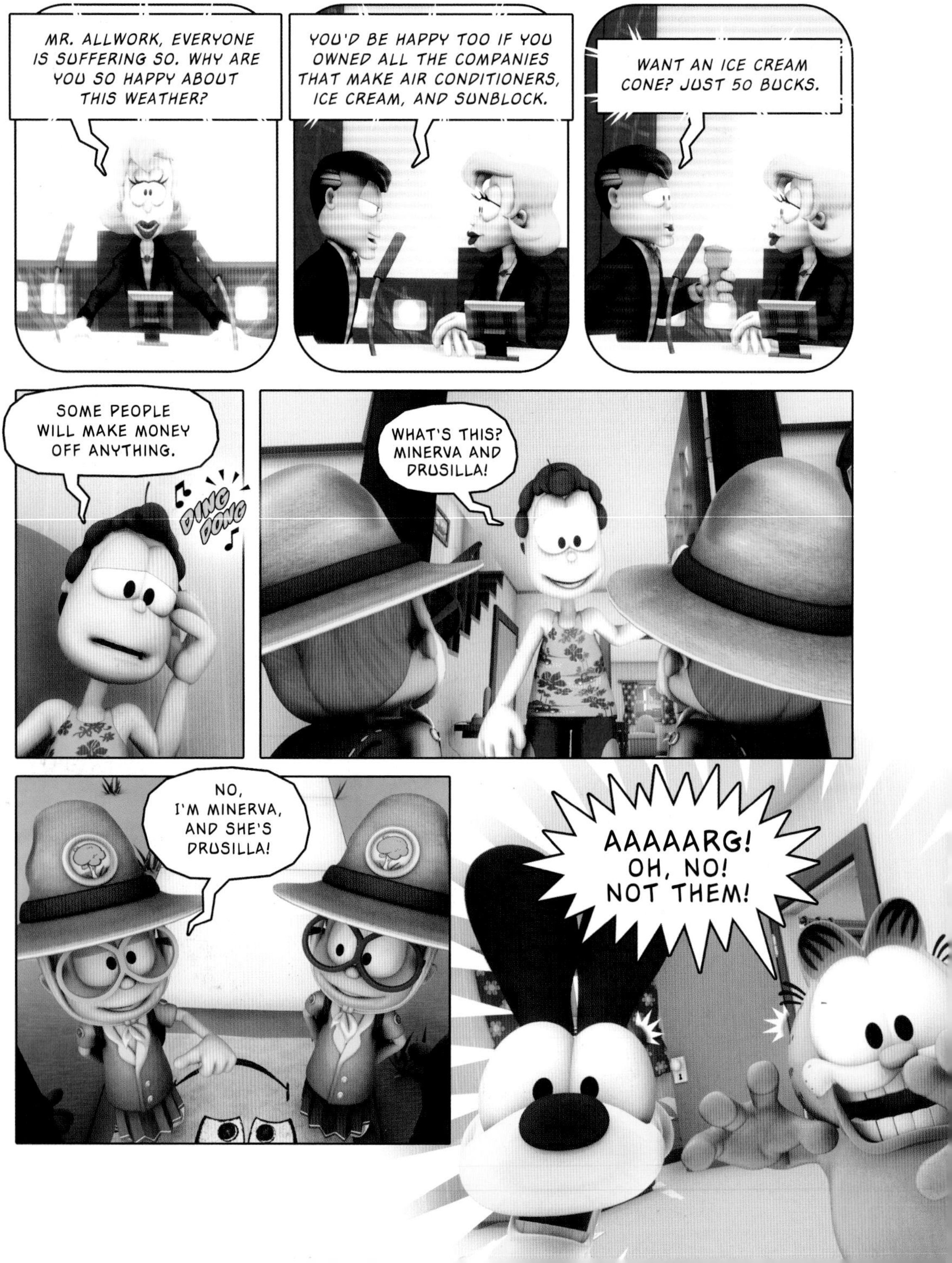
MR. ALLWORK, EVERYONE IS SUFFERING SO. WHY ARE YOU SO HAPPY ABOUT THIS WEATHER?
YOU'D BE HAPPY TOO IF YOU OWNED ALL THE COMPANIES THAT MAKE AIR CONDITIONERS, ICE CREAM, AND SUNBLOCK.
WANT AN ICE CREAM CONE? JUST 50 BUCKS.
SOME PEOPLE WILL MAKE MONEY OFF ANYTHING.
DING DONG
WHAT'S THIS? MINERVA AND DRUSILLA!
NO, I'M MINERVA, AND SHE'S DRUSILLA!
AAAAARG! OH, NO! NOT THEM!

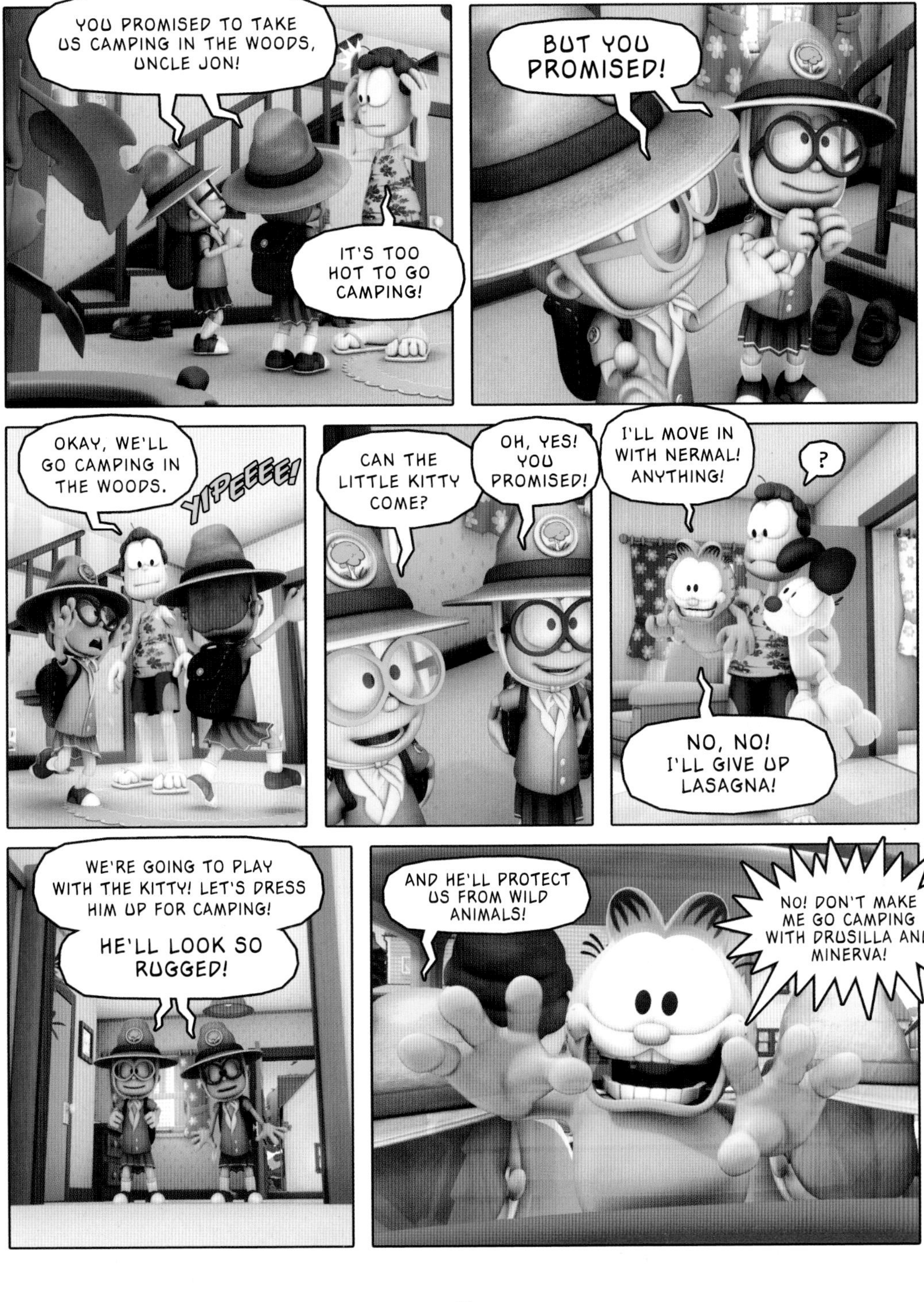

YOU PROMISED TO TAKE US CAMPING IN THE WOODS, UNCLE JON!
IT'S TOO HOT TO GO CAMPING!
BUT YOU PROMISED!
OKAY, WE'LL GO CAMPING IN THE WOODS.
YIPEEEE!
CAN THE LITTLE KITTY COME?
OH, YES! YOU PROMISED!
I'LL MOVE IN WITH NERMAL! ANYTHING!
?
NO, NO! I'LL GIVE UP LASAGNA!
WE'RE GOING TO PLAY WITH THE KITTY! LET'S DRESS HIM UP FOR CAMPING!
HE'LL LOOK SO RUGGED!
AND HE'LL PROTECT US FROM WILD ANIMALS!
NO! DON'T MAKE ME GO CAMPING WITH DRUSILLA AND MINERVA!

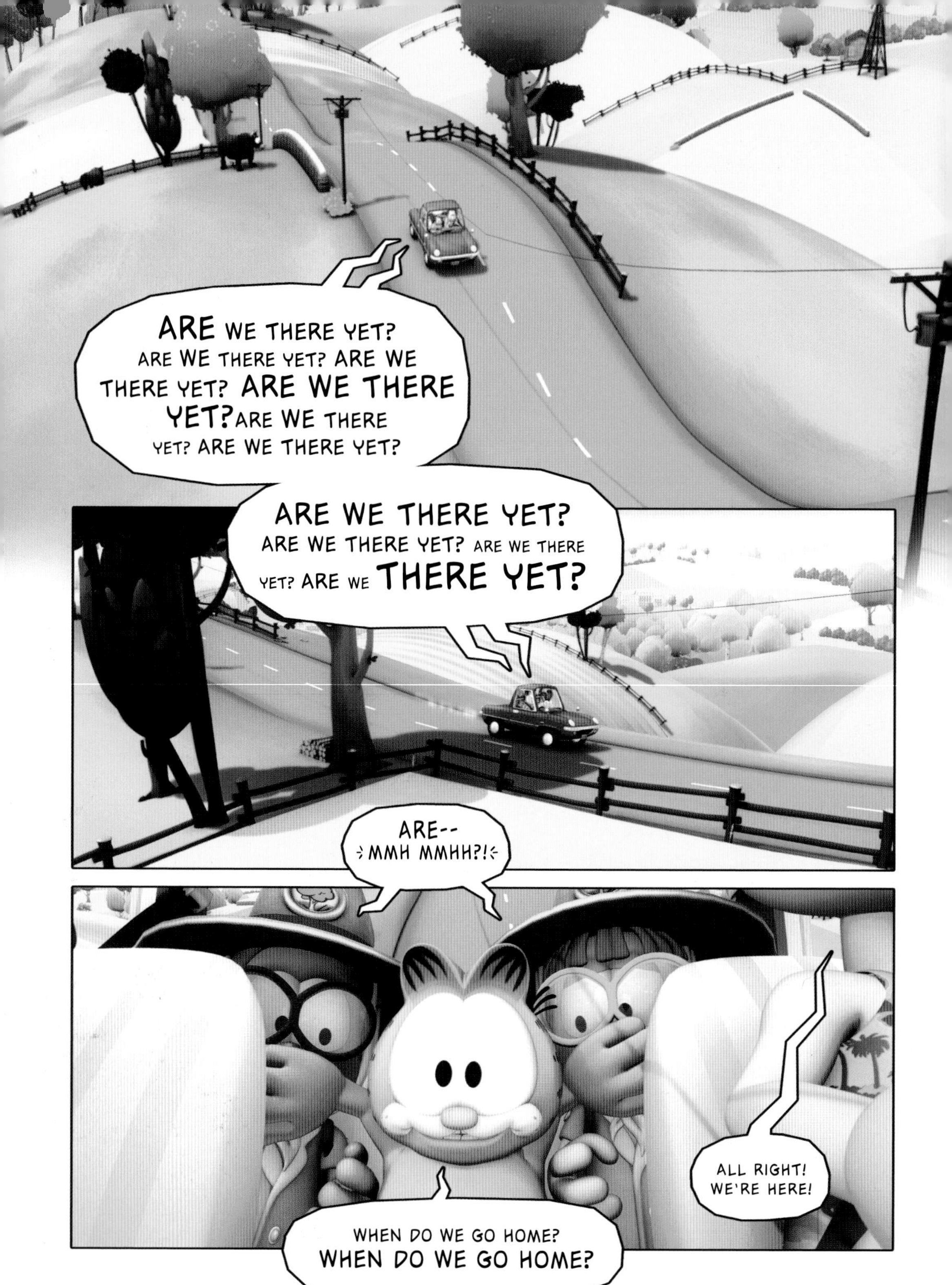

ARE WE THERE YET? ARE WE THERE YET? ARE WE THERE YET? ARE WE THERE YET?ARE WE THERE YET? ARE WE THERE YET?
ARE WE THERE YET? ARE WE THERE YET? ARE WE THERE YET? ARE WE THERE YET?
ARE-- MMH MMHH?!
ALL RIGHT! WE'RE HERE!
WHEN DO WE GO HOME? WHEN DO WE GO HOME?

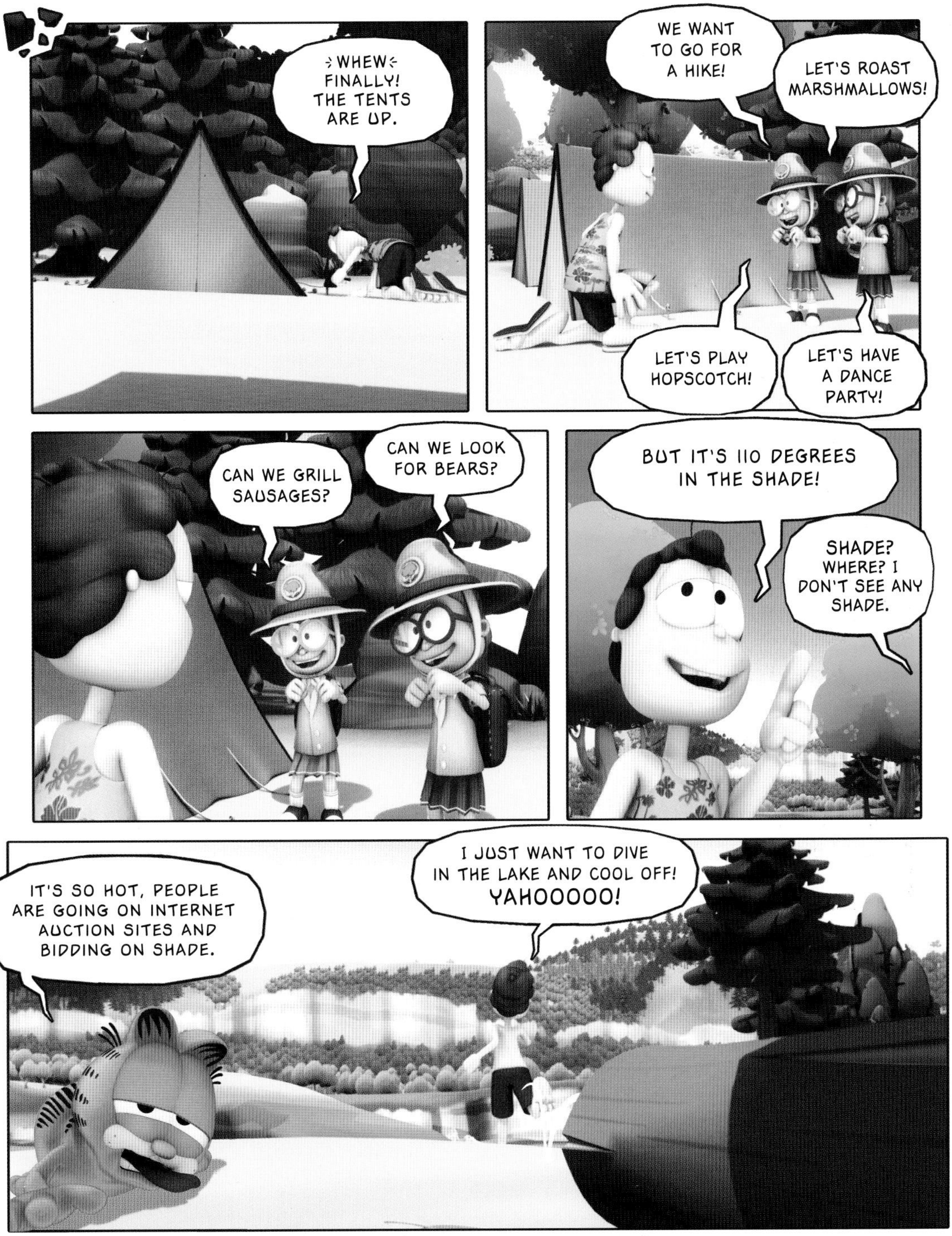
WHEW
FINALLY! THE TENTS ARE UP.
WE WANT TO GO FOR A HIKE!
LET'S ROAST MARSHMALLOWS!
LET'S PLAY HOPSCOTCH!
LET'S HAVE A DANCE PARTY!
CAN WE GRILL SAUSAGES?
CAN WE LOOK FOR BEARS?
BUT IT'S 110 DEGREES IN THE SHADE!
SHADE? WHERE? I DON'T SEE ANY SHADE.
IT'S SO HOT, PEOPLE ARE GOING ON INTERNET AUCTION SITES AND BIDDING ON SHADE.
I JUST WANT TO DIVE IN THE LAKE AND COOL OFF! YAHOOOOO!

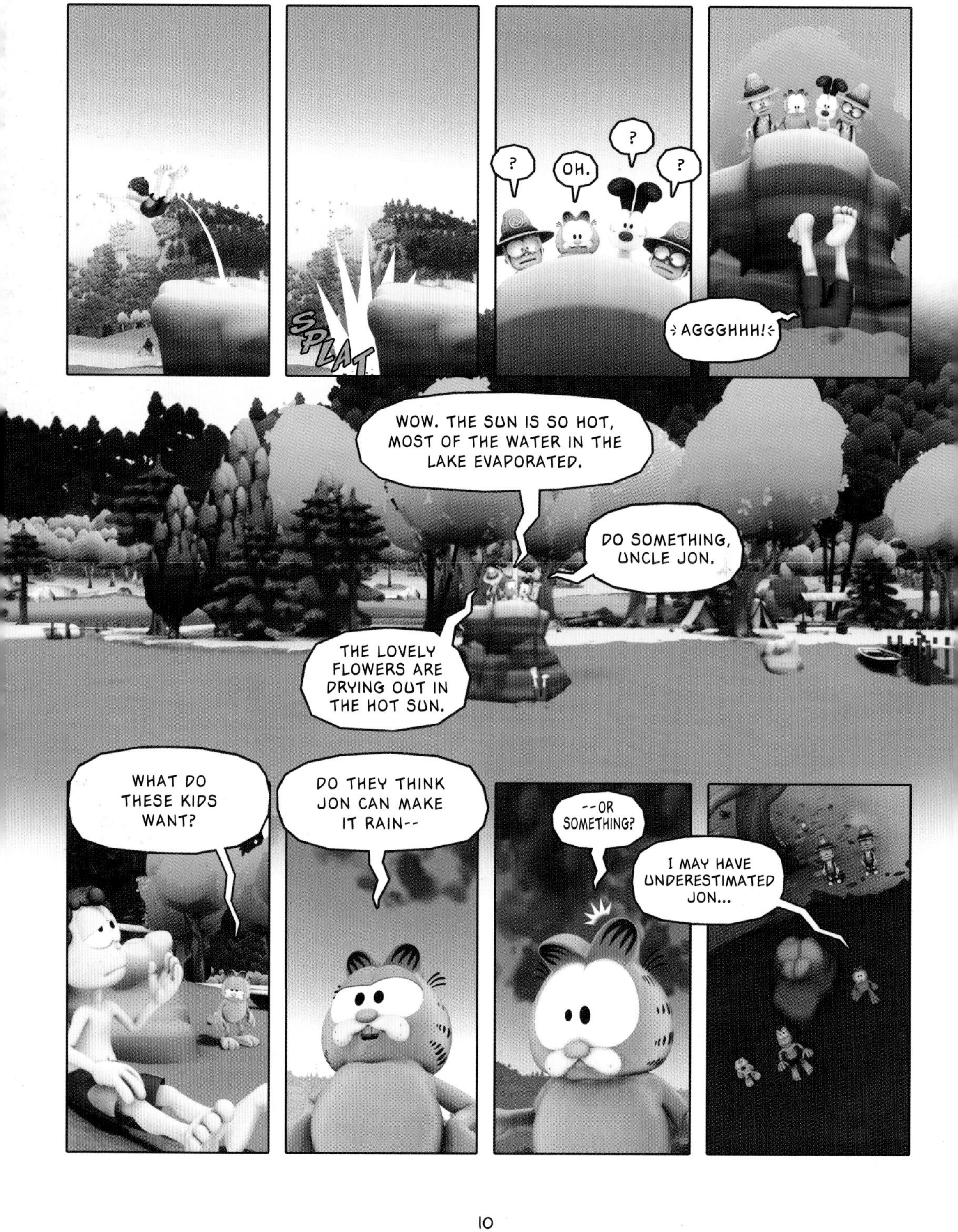
SPLAT
?
OH.
?
?
AGGGHHH!
WOW. THE SUN IS SO HOT, MOST OF THE WATER IN THE LAKE EVAPORATED.
DO SOMETHING, UNCLE JON.
THE LOVELY FLOWERS ARE DRYING OUT IN THE HOT SUN.
WHAT DO THESE KIDS WANT?
DO THEY THINK JON CAN MAKE IT RAIN--
--OR SOMETHING?
I MAY HAVE UNDERESTIMATED JON...

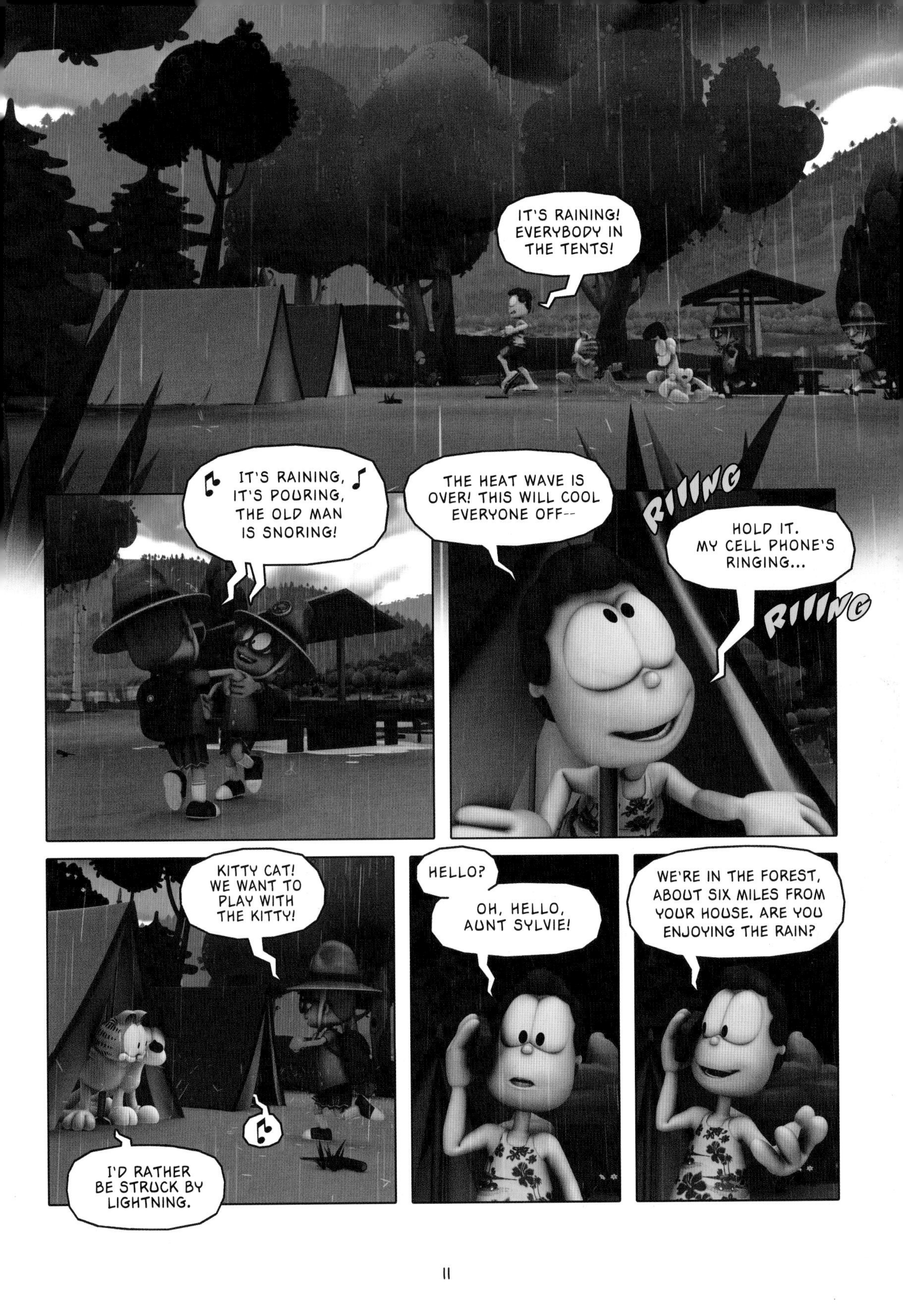
IT'S RAINING! EVERYBODY IN THE TENTS!
IT'S RAINING, IT'S POURING, THE OLD MAN IS SNORING!
THE HEAT WAVE IS OVER! THIS WILL COOL EVERYONE OFF--
RIIING
HOLD IT. MY CELL PHONE'S RINGING...
RIIING
KITTY CAT! WE WANT TO PLAY WITH THE KITTY!
I'D RATHER BE STRUCK BY LIGHTNING.
HELLO?
OH, HELLO, AUNT SYLVIE!
WE'RE IN THE FOREST, ABOUT SIX MILES FROM YOUR HOUSE. ARE YOU ENJOYING THE RAIN?

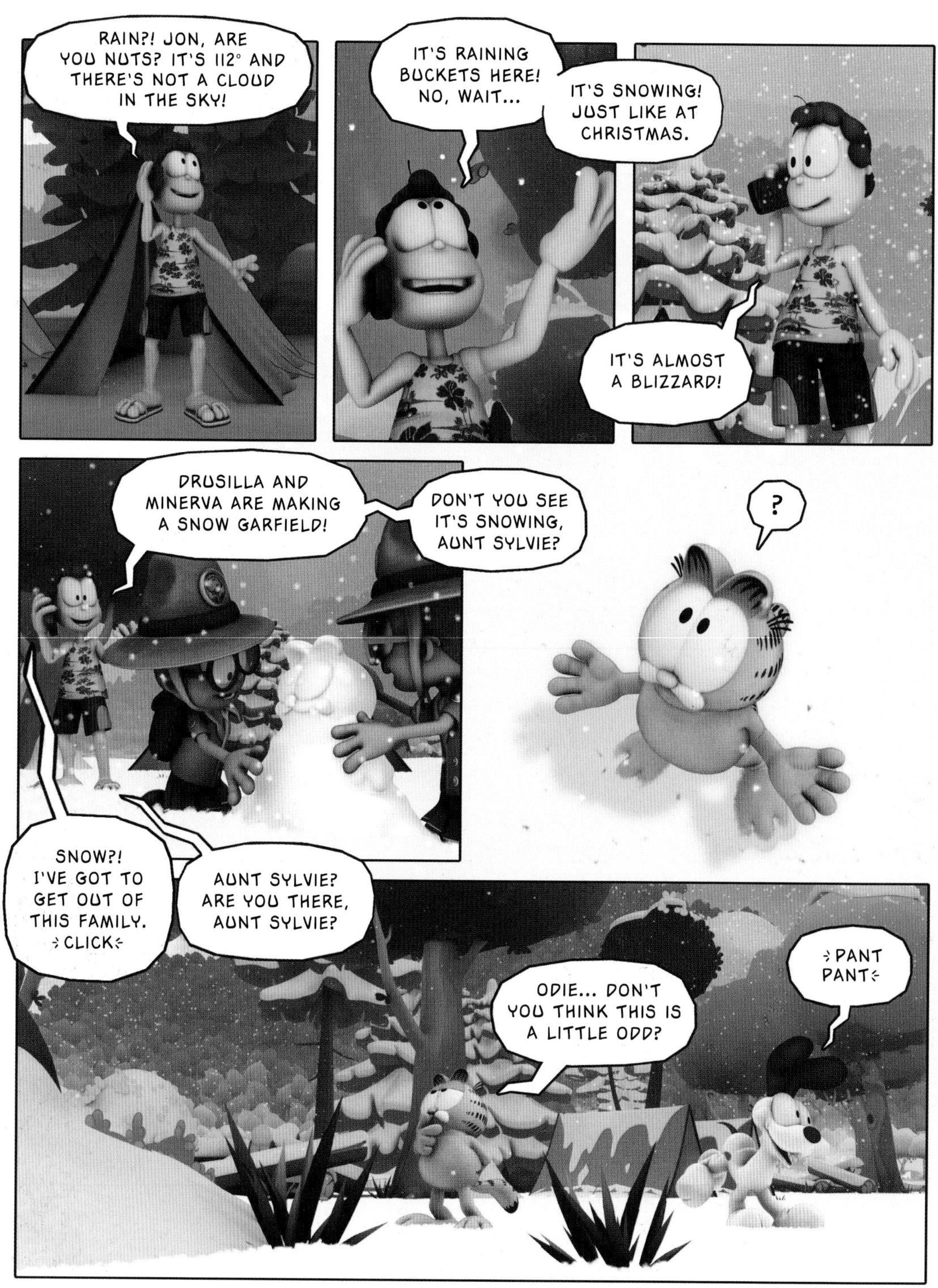

RAIN?! JON, ARE YOU NUTS? IT'S 112° AND THERE'S NOT A CLOUD IN THE SKY!
IT'S RAINING BUCKETS HERE! NO, WAIT...
IT'S SNOWING! JUST LIKE AT CHRISTMAS.
IT'S ALMOST A BLIZZARD!
DRUSILLA AND MINERVA ARE MAKING A SNOW GARFIELD!
DON'T YOU SEE IT'S SNOWING, AUNT SYLVIE?
?
SNOW?! I'VE GOT TO GET OUT OF THIS FAMILY. CLICK
AUNT SYLVIE? ARE YOU THERE, AUNT SYLVIE?
ODIE... DON'T YOU THINK THIS IS A LITTLE ODD?
PANT PANT

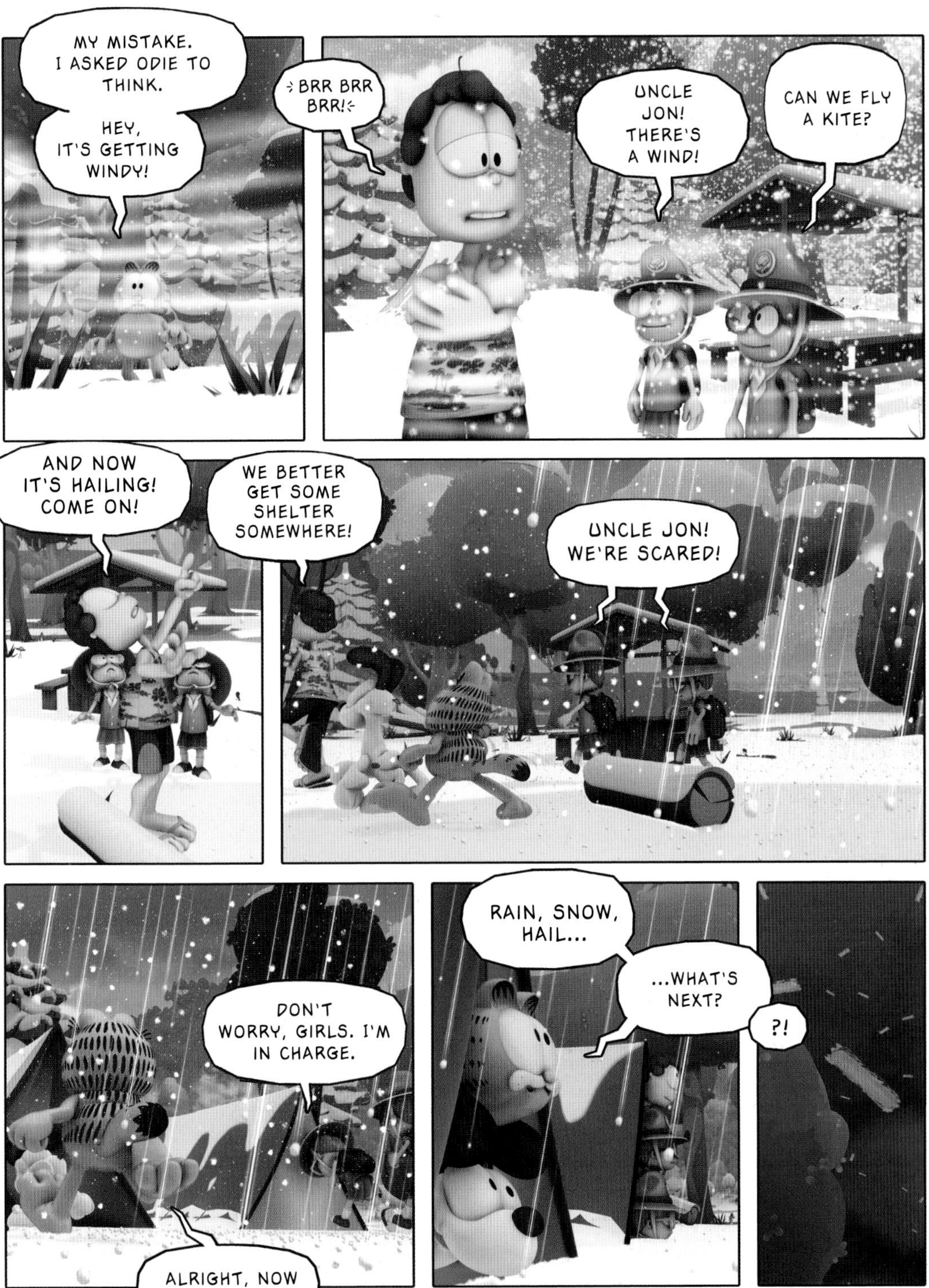
MY MISTAKE. I ASKED ODIE TO THINK.
HEY, IT'S GETTING WINDY!
BRR BRR BRR!
UNCLE JON! THERE'S A WIND!
CAN WE FLY A KITE?
AND NOW IT'S HAILING! COME ON!
WE BETTER GET SOME SHELTER SOMEWHERE!
UNCLE JON! WE'RE SCARED!
DON'T WORRY, GIRLS. I'M IN CHARGE.
ALRIGHT, NOW I'M SCARED.
RAIN, SNOW, HAIL...
...WHAT'S NEXT?
?!

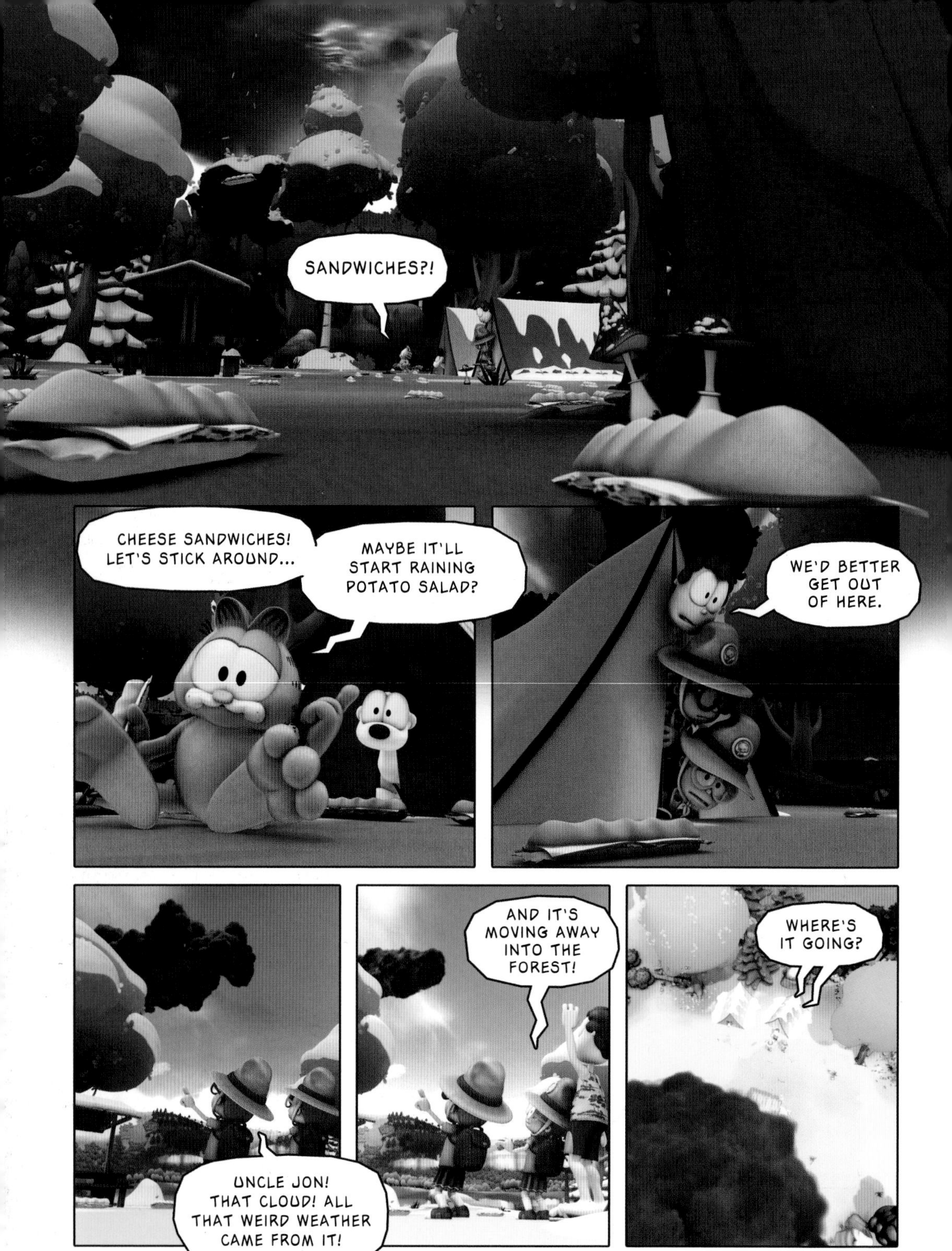
SANDWICHES?!
CHEESE SANDWICHES! LET'S STICK AROUND...
MAYBE IT'LL START RAINING POTATO SALAD?
WE'D BETTER GET OUT OF HERE.
UNCLE JON! THAT CLOUD! ALL THAT WEIRD WEATHER CAME FROM IT!
AND IT'S MOVING AWAY INTO THE FOREST!
WHERE'S IT GOING?

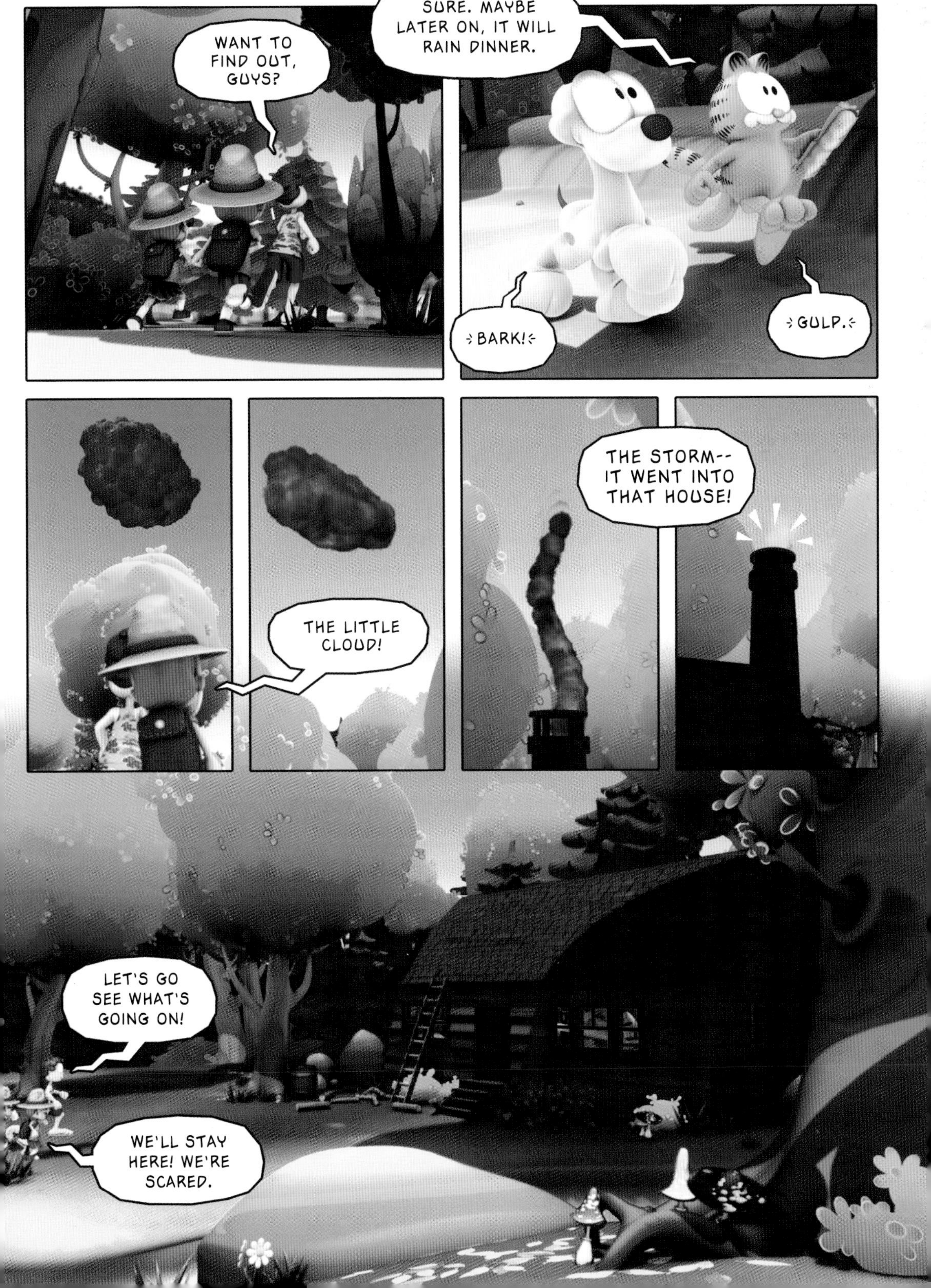
WANT TO FIND OUT, GUYS?
SURE. MAYBE LATER ON, IT WILL RAIN DINNER.
BARK!
GULP.
THE LITTLE CLOUD!
THE STORM-- IT WENT INTO THAT HOUSE!
LET'S GO SEE WHAT'S GOING ON!
WE'LL STAY HERE! WE'RE SCARED.

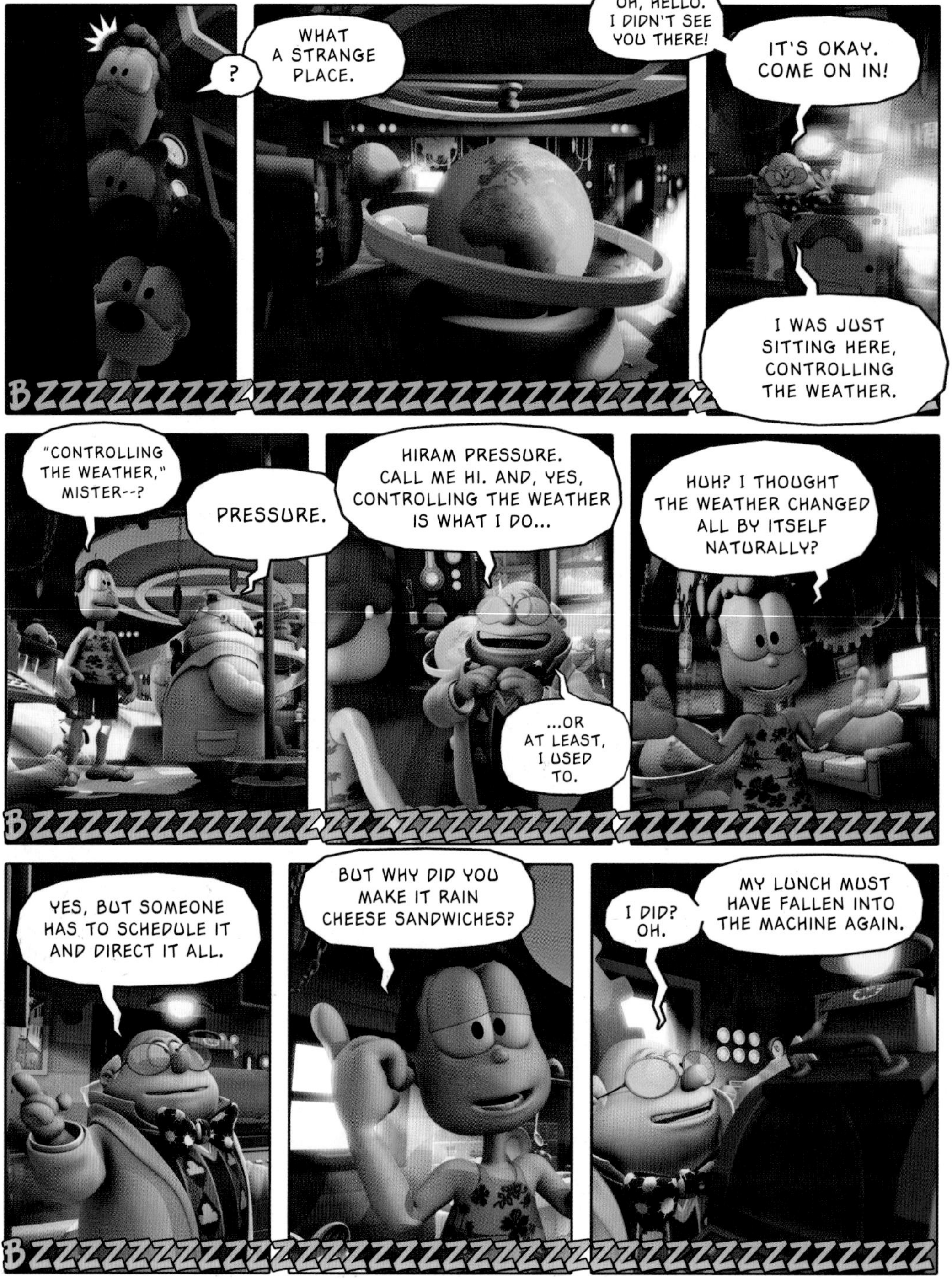
?
WHAT A STRANGE PLACE.
OH, HELLO. I DIDN'T SEE YOU THERE!
IT'S OKAY. COME ON IN!
I WAS JUST SITTING HERE, CONTROLLING THE WEATHER.
BZZZZZZZZZZZZZZZZZZZZZZZZZZZZZZZZZZZ
"CONTROLLING THE WEATHER," MISTER--?
PRESSURE.
HIRAM PRESSURE. CALL ME HI. AND, YES, CONTROLLING THE WEATHER IS WHAT I DO...
...OR AT LEAST, I USED TO.
HUH? I THOUGHT THE WEATHER CHANGED ALL BY ITSELF NATURALLY?
BZZZZZZZZZZZZZZZZZZZZZZZZZZZZZZZZZZZZZZZZZZZZZ
YES, BUT SOMEONE HAS TO SCHEDULE IT AND DIRECT IT ALL.
BUT WHY DID YOU MAKE IT RAIN CHEESE SANDWICHES?
I DID? OH.
MY LUNCH MUST HAVE FALLEN INTO THE MACHINE AGAIN.
BZZZZZZZZZZZZZZZZZZZZZZZZZZZZZZZZZZZZZZZZZZZZZ

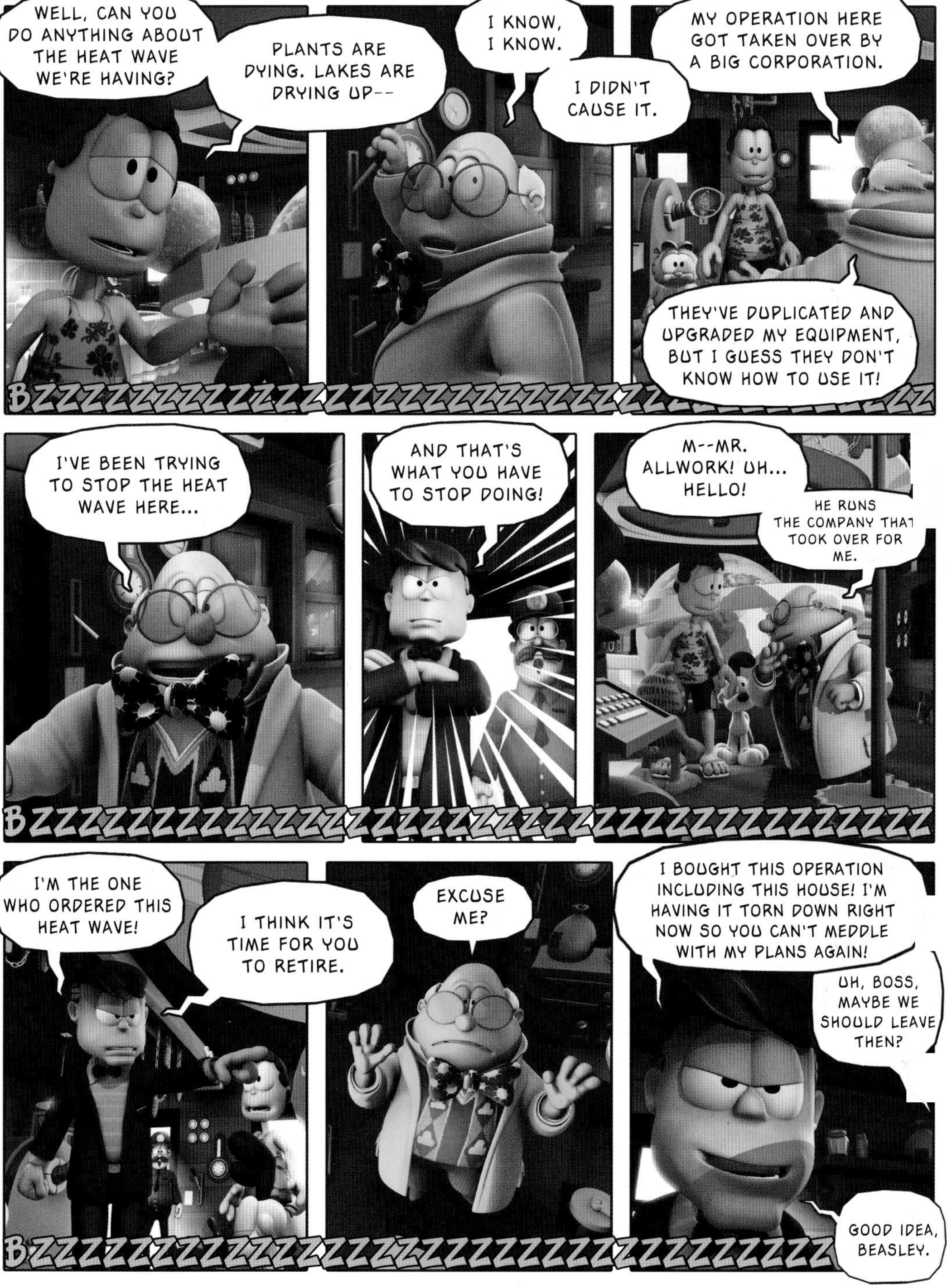
WELL, CAN YOU DO ANYTHING ABOUT THE HEAT WAVE WE'RE HAVING?
PLANTS ARE DYING. LAKES ARE DRYING UP--
I KNOW, I KNOW.
I DIDN'T CAUSE IT.
MY OPERATION HERE GOT TAKEN OVER BY A BIG CORPORATION.
THEY'VE DUPLICATED AND UPGRADED MY EQUIPMENT, BUT I GUESS THEY DON'T KNOW HOW TO USE IT!
BZZZZZZZZZZZZZZZZZZZZZZZZZZZZZZ
I'VE BEEN TRYING TO STOP THE HEAT WAVE HERE...
AND THAT'S WHAT YOU HAVE TO STOP DOING!
M--MR. ALLWORK! UH... HELLO!
HE RUNS THE COMPANY THAT TOOK OVER FOR ME.
BZZZZZZZZZZZZZZZZZZZZZZZZZZZZZZZZZZZZZZZZZ
I'M THE ONE WHO ORDERED THIS HEAT WAVE!
I THINK IT'S TIME FOR YOU TO RETIRE.
EXCUSE ME?
I BOUGHT THIS OPERATION INCLUDING THIS HOUSE! I'M HAVING IT TORN DOWN RIGHT NOW SO YOU CAN'T MEDDLE WITH MY PLANS AGAIN!
UH, BOSS, MAYBE WE SHOULD LEAVE THEN?
GOOD IDEA, BEASLEY.
BZZZZZZZZZZZZZZZZZZZZZZZZZZZZZZZZZZZZZZ

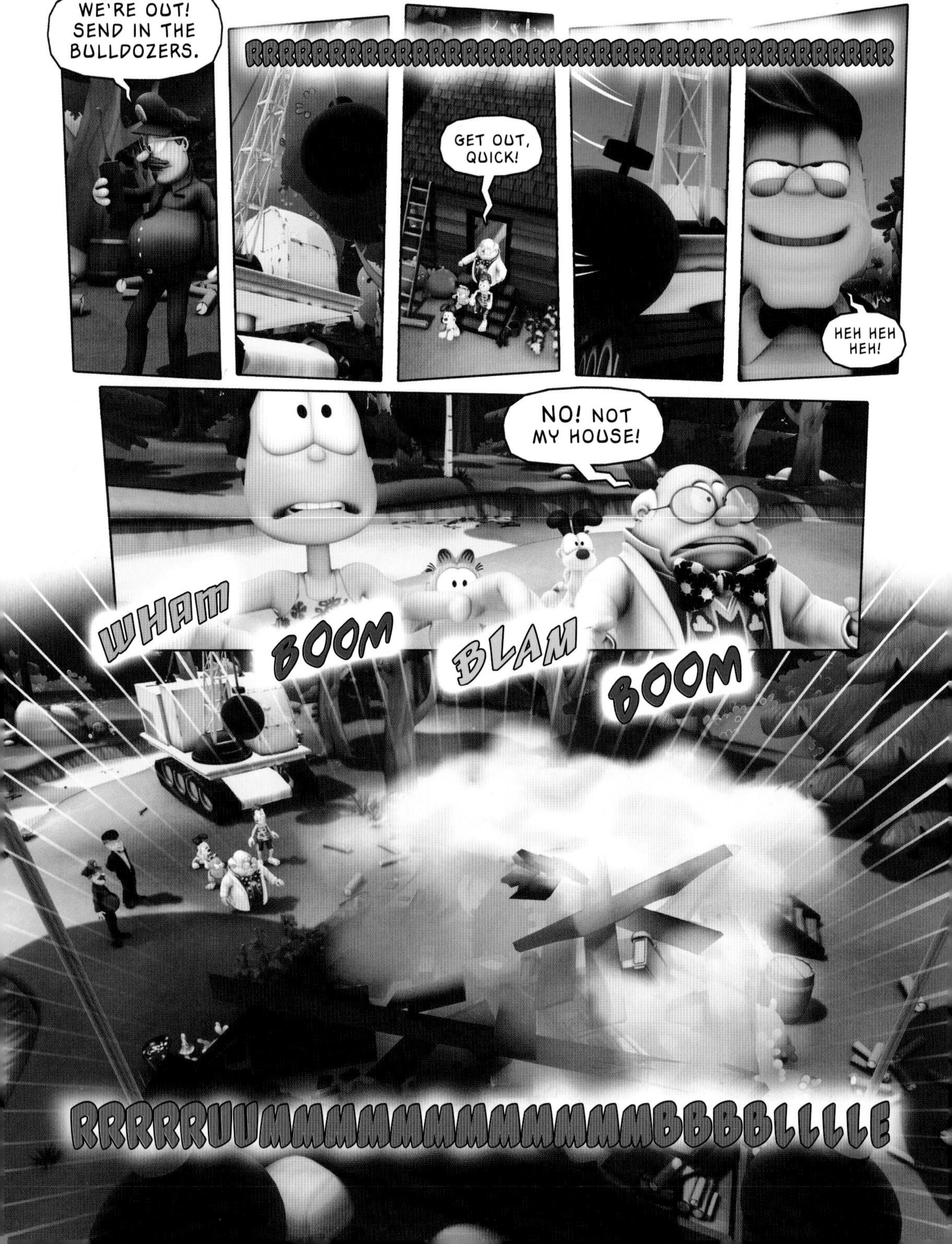
WE'RE OUT! SEND IN THE BULLDOZERS.
RRRRRRRRRRRRRRRRRRRRRRRRRRRRRRRRRRRRRRRR
GET OUT, QUICK!
HEH HEH HEH!
NO! NOT MY HOUSE!
WHAM
BOOM
BLAM
BOOM
RRRRRUUMMMMMMMMMMMMMMMBBBBLLLLE

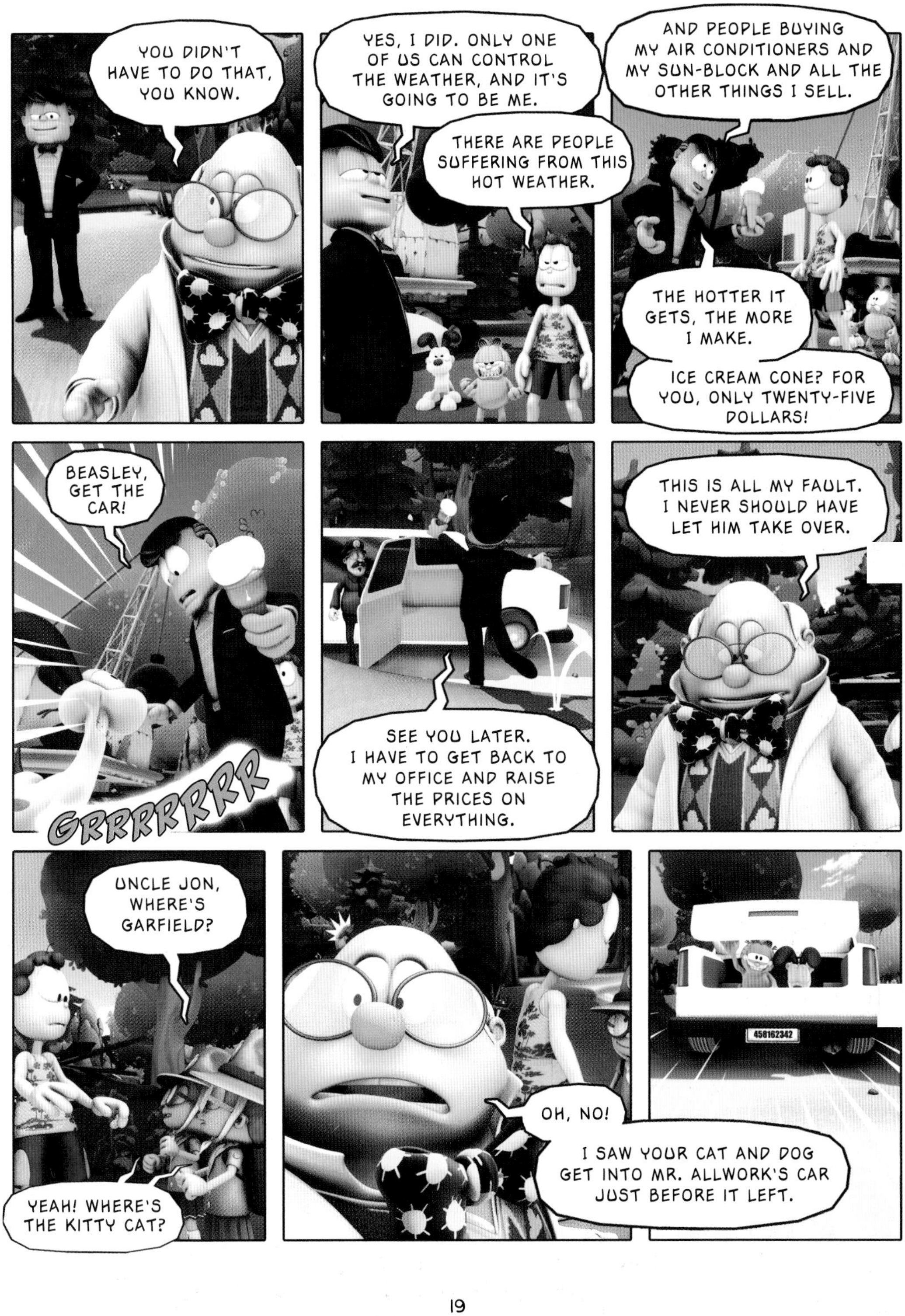
YOU DIDN'T HAVE TO DO THAT, YOU KNOW.
YES, I DID. ONLY ONE OF US CAN CONTROL THE WEATHER, AND IT'S GOING TO BE ME.
THERE ARE PEOPLE SUFFERING FROM THIS HOT WEATHER.
AND PEOPLE BUYING MY AIR CONDITIONERS AND MY SUN-BLOCK AND ALL THE OTHER THINGS I SELL.
THE HOTTER IT GETS, THE MORE I MAKE.
ICE CREAM CONE? FOR YOU, ONLY TWENTY-FIVE DOLLARS!
BEASLEY, GET THE CAR!
GRRRRRRR
SEE YOU LATER. I HAVE TO GET BACK TO MY OFFICE AND RAISE THE PRICES ON EVERYTHING.
THIS IS ALL MY FAULT. I NEVER SHOULD HAVE LET HIM TAKE OVER.
UNCLE JON, WHERE'S GARFIELD?
YEAH! WHERE'S THE KITTY CAT?
OH, NO!
I SAW YOUR CAT AND DOG GET INTO MR. ALLWORK'S CAR JUST BEFORE IT LEFT.
458162342

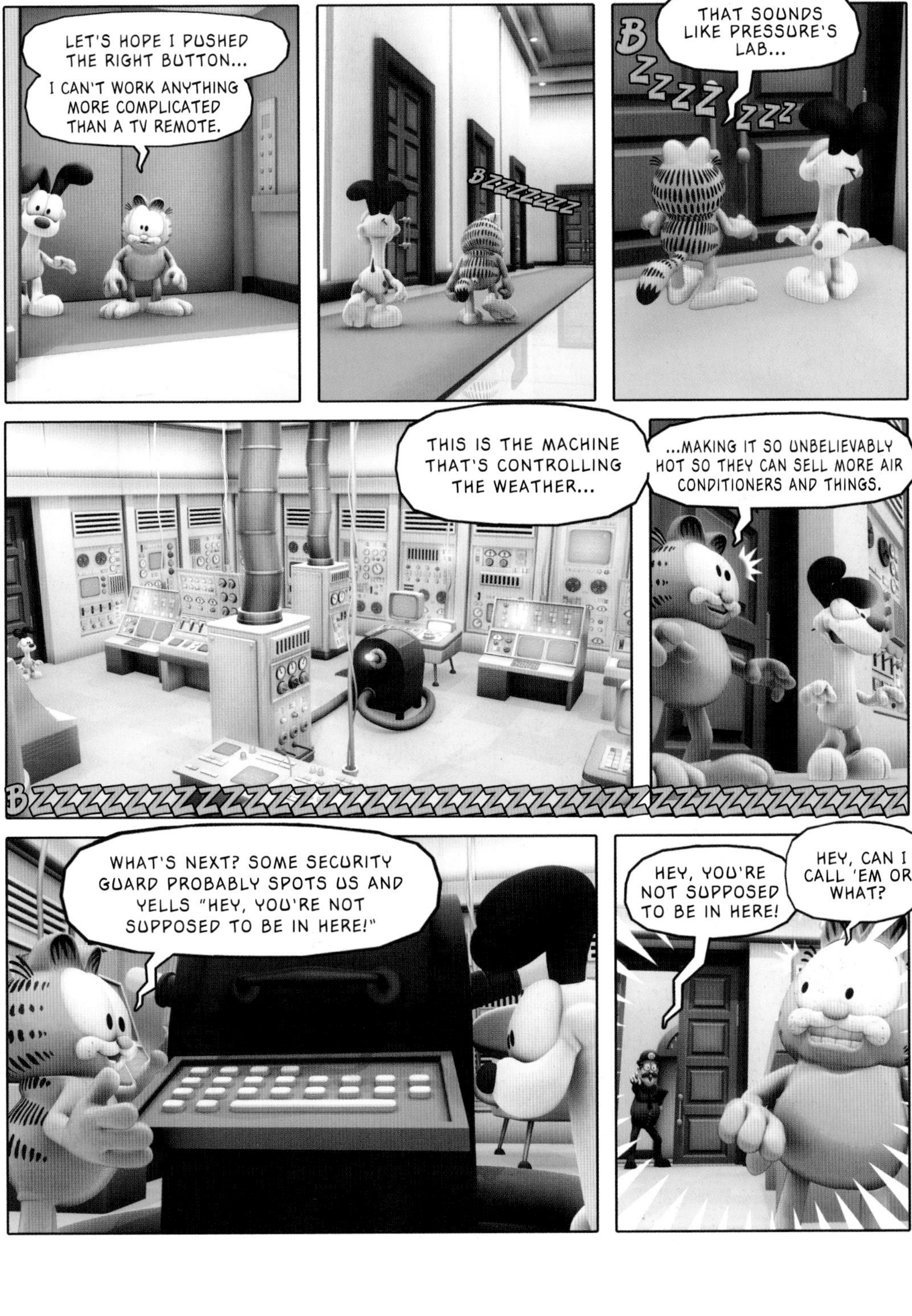
LET'S HOPE I PUSHED THE RIGHT BUTTON...
I CAN'T WORK ANYTHING MORE COMPLICATED THAN A TV REMOTE.
BZZZZZZZZ
BZZZZZZZ
THAT SOUNDS LIKE PRESSURE'S LAB...
THIS IS THE MACHINE THAT'S CONTROLLING THE WEATHER...
...MAKING IT SO UNBELIEVABLY HOT SO THEY CAN SELL MORE AIR CONDITIONERS AND THINGS.
BZZZZZZZZZZZZZZZZZZZZZZZZZZZZZZZZZZZZZZZZZZZZZZZZZZZZZ
WHAT'S NEXT? SOME SECURITY GUARD PROBABLY SPOTS US AND YELLS "HEY, YOU'RE NOT SUPPOSED TO BE IN HERE!"
HEY, YOU'RE NOT SUPPOSED TO BE IN HERE!
HEY, CAN I CALL 'EM OR WHAT?

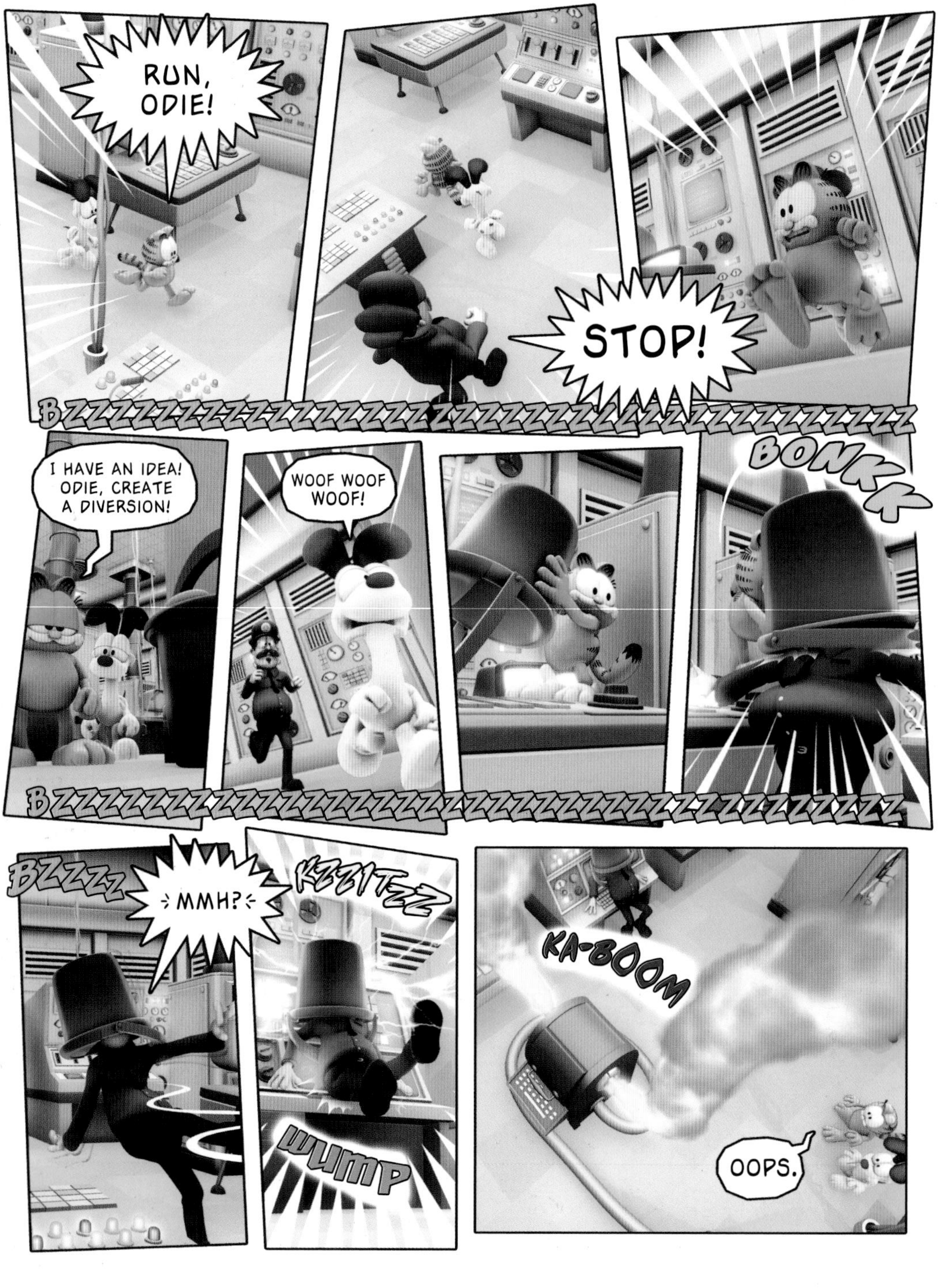

RUN, ODIE!
STOP!
BZZZZZZZZZZZZZZZZZZZZZZZZZZZZZZZZZZZ
I HAVE AN IDEA! ODIE, CREATE A DIVERSION!
WOOF WOOF WOOF!
BONKK
BZZZZZZZZZZZZZZZZZZZZZZZZZZZZZZZZZZZ
BZZZZ
MMH?
WUMP
KA-BOOM
OOPS.

23

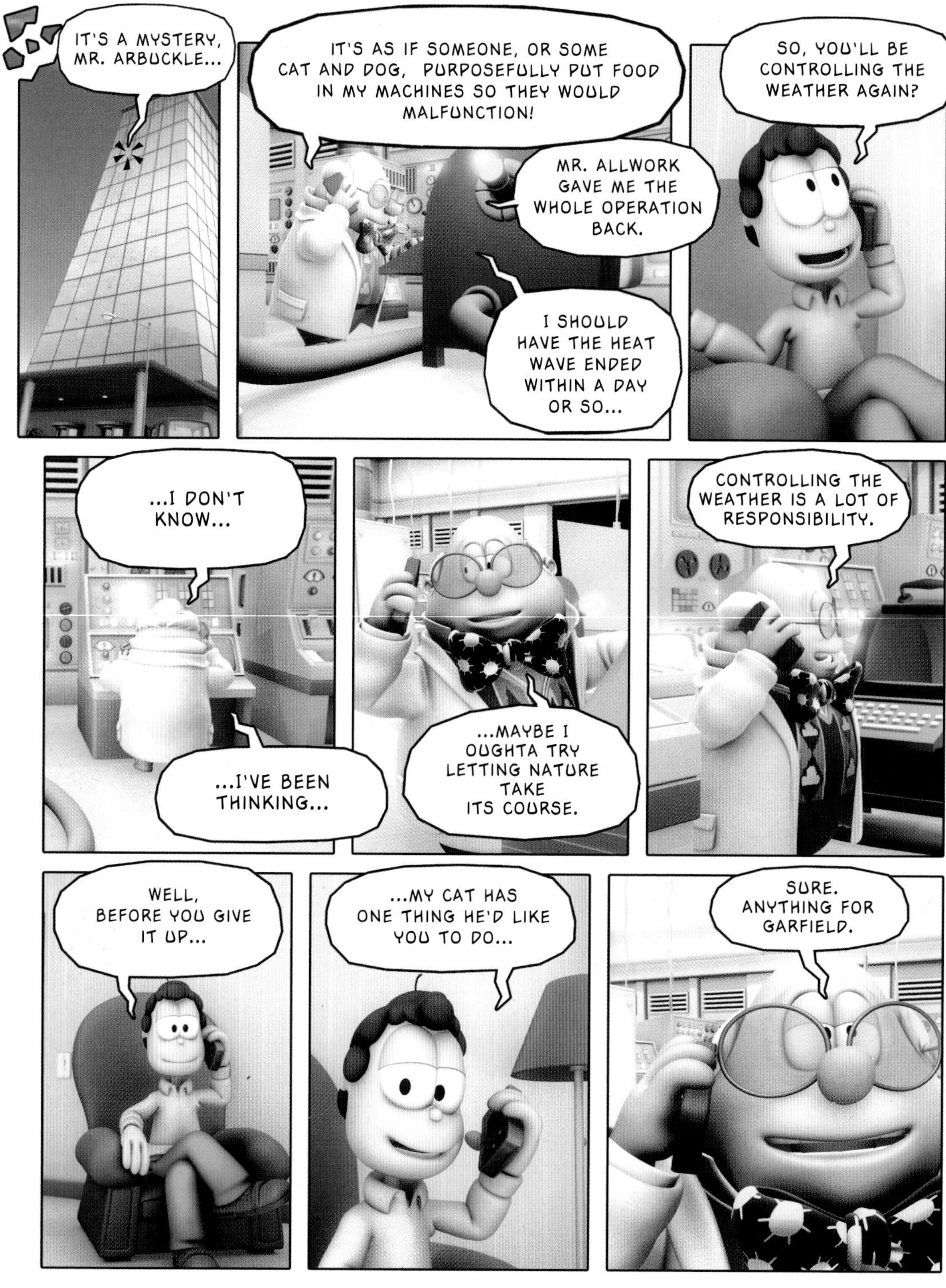

IT'S A MYSTERY, MR. ARBUCKLE...
IT'S AS IF SOMEONE, OR SOME CAT AND DOG, PURPOSEFULLY PUT FOOD IN MY MACHINES SO THEY WOULD MALFUNCTION!
MR. ALLWORK GAVE ME THE WHOLE OPERATION BACK.
I SHOULD HAVE THE HEAT WAVE ENDED WITHIN A DAY OR SO...
SO, YOU'LL BE CONTROLLING THE WEATHER AGAIN?
...I DON'T KNOW...
...I'VE BEEN THINKING...
...MAYBE I OUGHTA TRY LETTING NATURE TAKE ITS COURSE.
CONTROLLING THE WEATHER IS A LOT OF RESPONSIBILITY.
WELL, BEFORE YOU GIVE IT UP...
...MY CAT HAS ONE THING HE'D LIKE YOU TO DO...
SURE. ANYTHING FOR GARFIELD.

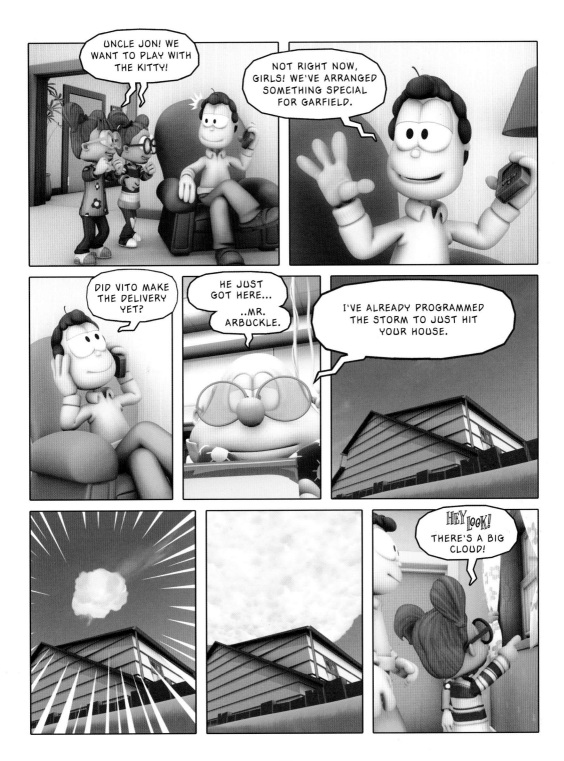

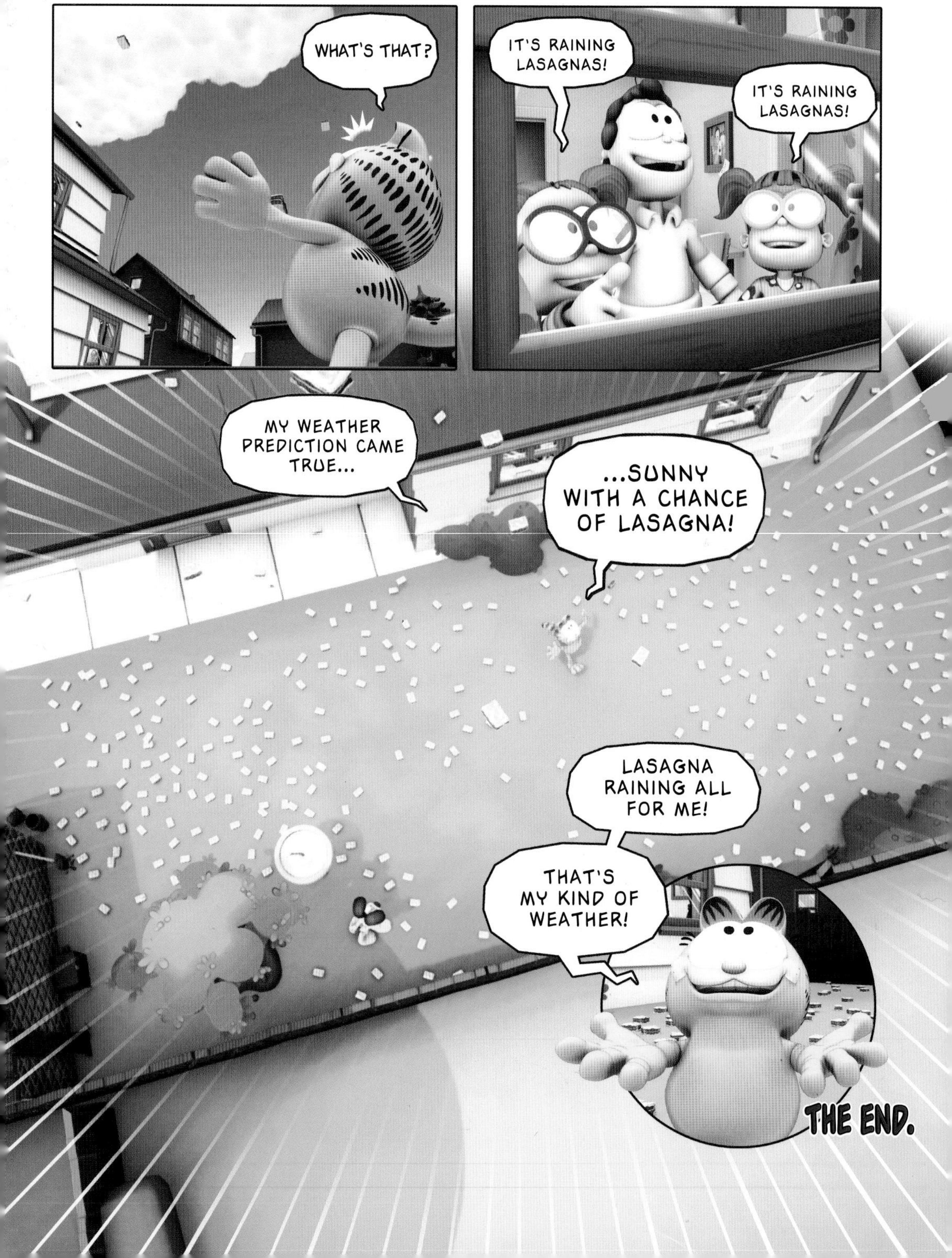
WHAT'S THAT?
IT'S RAINING LASAGNAS!
IT'S RAINING LASAGNAS!
MY WEATHER PREDICTION CAME TRUE...
...SUNNY WITH A CHANCE OF LASAGNA!
LASAGNA RAINING ALL FOR ME!
THAT'S MY KIND OF WEATHER!
THE END.

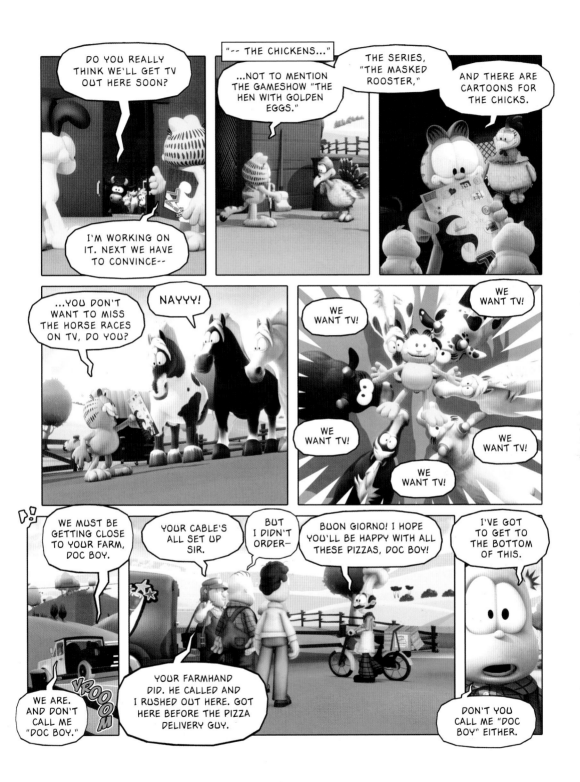

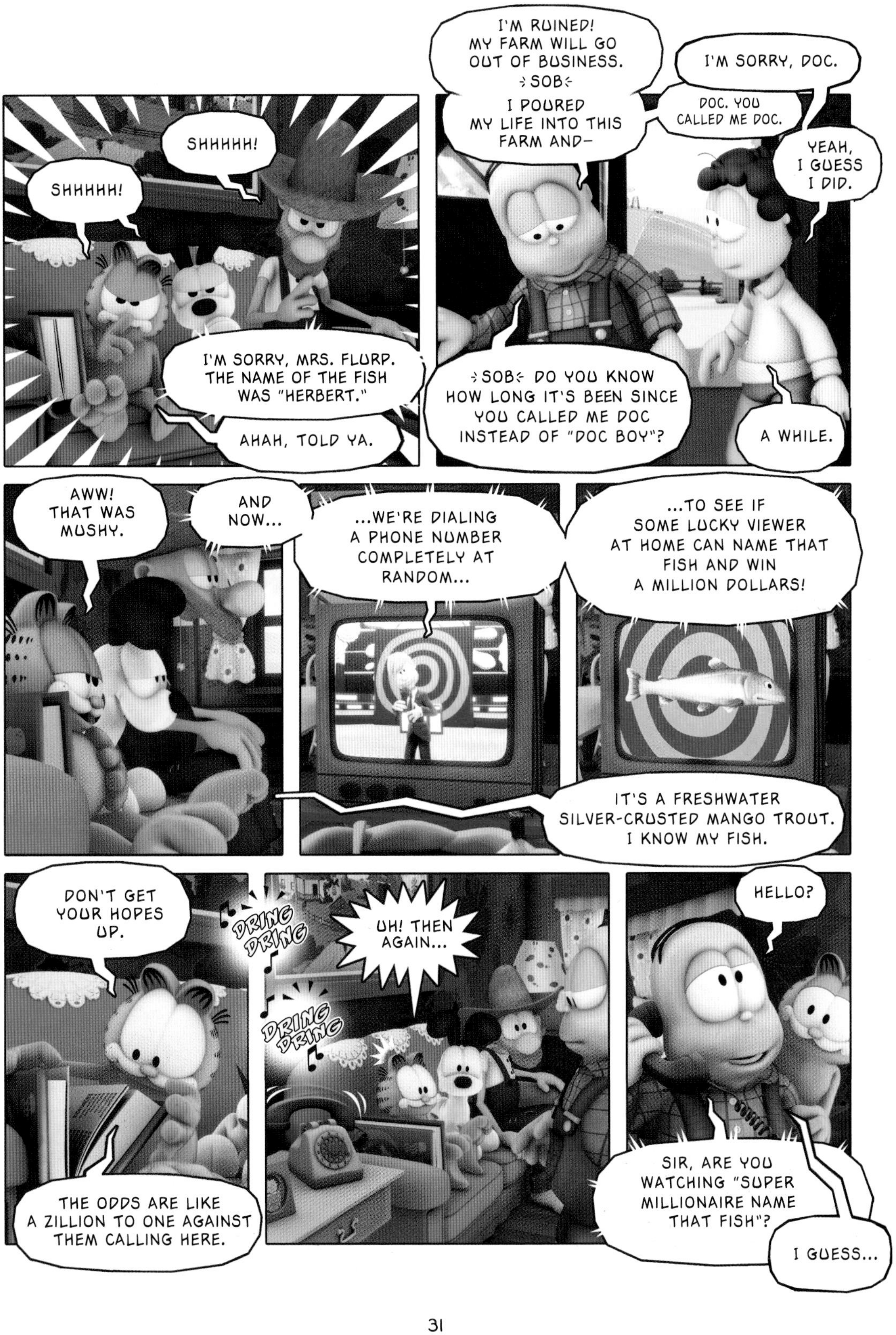
SHHHHH!
SHHHHH!
I'M SORRY, MRS. FLURP. THE NAME OF THE FISH WAS "HERBERT."
AHAH, TOLD YA.
I'M RUINED! MY FARM WILL GO OUT OF BUSINESS. ⊰SOB⊱
I POURED MY LIFE INTO THIS FARM AND–
I'M SORRY, DOC.
DOC. YOU CALLED ME DOC.
YEAH, I GUESS I DID.
⊰SOB⊱ DO YOU KNOW HOW LONG IT'S BEEN SINCE YOU CALLED ME DOC INSTEAD OF "DOC BOY"?
A WHILE.
AWW! THAT WAS MUSHY.
AND NOW...
...WE'RE DIALING A PHONE NUMBER COMPLETELY AT RANDOM...
...TO SEE IF SOME LUCKY VIEWER AT HOME CAN NAME THAT FISH AND WIN A MILLION DOLLARS!
IT'S A FRESHWATER SILVER-CRUSTED MANGO TROUT. I KNOW MY FISH.
DON'T GET YOUR HOPES UP.
THE ODDS ARE LIKE A ZILLION TO ONE AGAINST THEM CALLING HERE.
DRING DRING
UH! THEN AGAIN...
DRING DRING
HELLO?
SIR, ARE YOU WATCHING "SUPER MILLIONAIRE NAME THAT FISH"?
I GUESS...

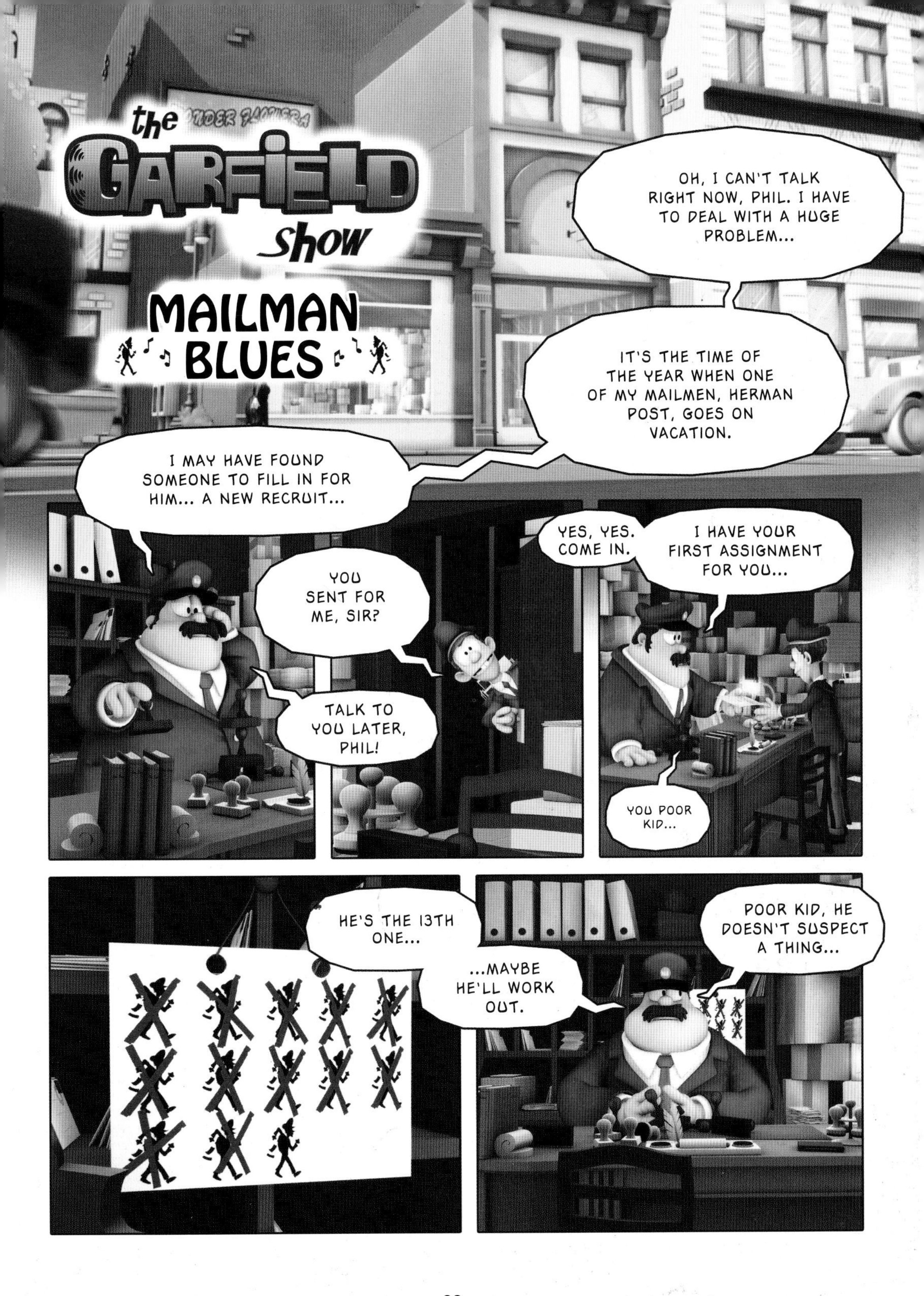
the GARFIELD show
MAILMAN BLUES
OH, I CAN'T TALK RIGHT NOW, PHIL. I HAVE TO DEAL WITH A HUGE PROBLEM...
IT'S THE TIME OF THE YEAR WHEN ONE OF MY MAILMEN, HERMAN POST, GOES ON VACATION.
I MAY HAVE FOUND SOMEONE TO FILL IN FOR HIM... A NEW RECRUIT...
YOU SENT FOR ME, SIR?
TALK TO YOU LATER, PHIL!
YES, YES. COME IN.
I HAVE YOUR FIRST ASSIGNMENT FOR YOU...
YOU POOR KID...
HE'S THE 13TH ONE...
...MAYBE HE'LL WORK OUT.
POOR KID, HE DOESN'T SUSPECT A THING...

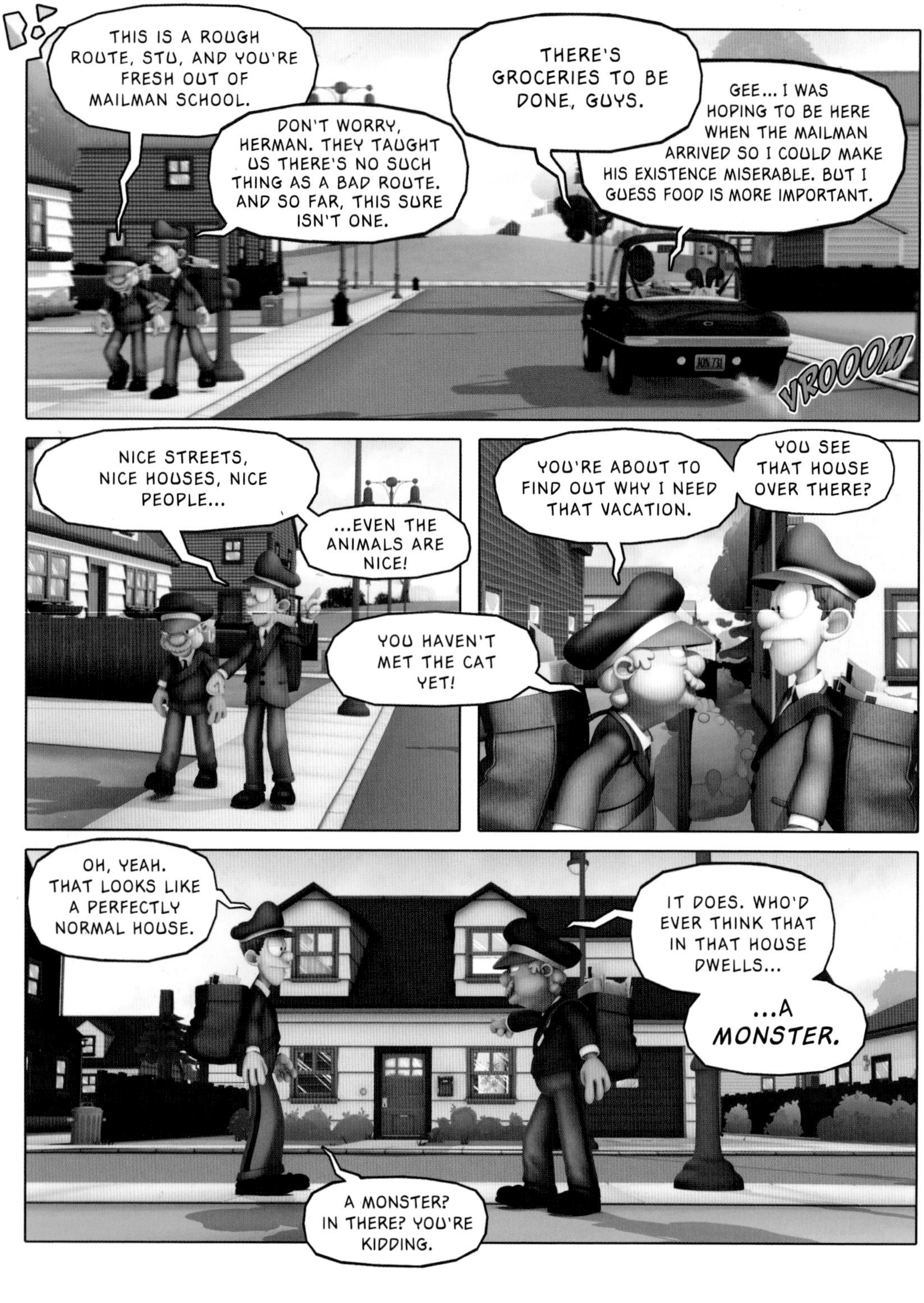

THIS IS A ROUGH ROUTE, STU, AND YOU'RE FRESH OUT OF MAILMAN SCHOOL.
DON'T WORRY, HERMAN. THEY TAUGHT US THERE'S NO SUCH THING AS A BAD ROUTE. AND SO FAR, THIS SURE ISN'T ONE.
THERE'S GROCERIES TO BE DONE, GUYS.
GEE... I WAS HOPING TO BE HERE WHEN THE MAILMAN ARRIVED SO I COULD MAKE HIS EXISTENCE MISERABLE. BUT I GUESS FOOD IS MORE IMPORTANT.
VROOOM
NICE STREETS, NICE HOUSES, NICE PEOPLE...
...EVEN THE ANIMALS ARE NICE!
YOU HAVEN'T MET THE CAT YET!
YOU'RE ABOUT TO FIND OUT WHY I NEED THAT VACATION.
YOU SEE THAT HOUSE OVER THERE?
OH, YEAH. THAT LOOKS LIKE A PERFECTLY NORMAL HOUSE.
IT DOES. WHO'D EVER THINK THAT IN THAT HOUSE DWELLS...
...A MONSTER.
A MONSTER? IN THERE? YOU'RE KIDDING.

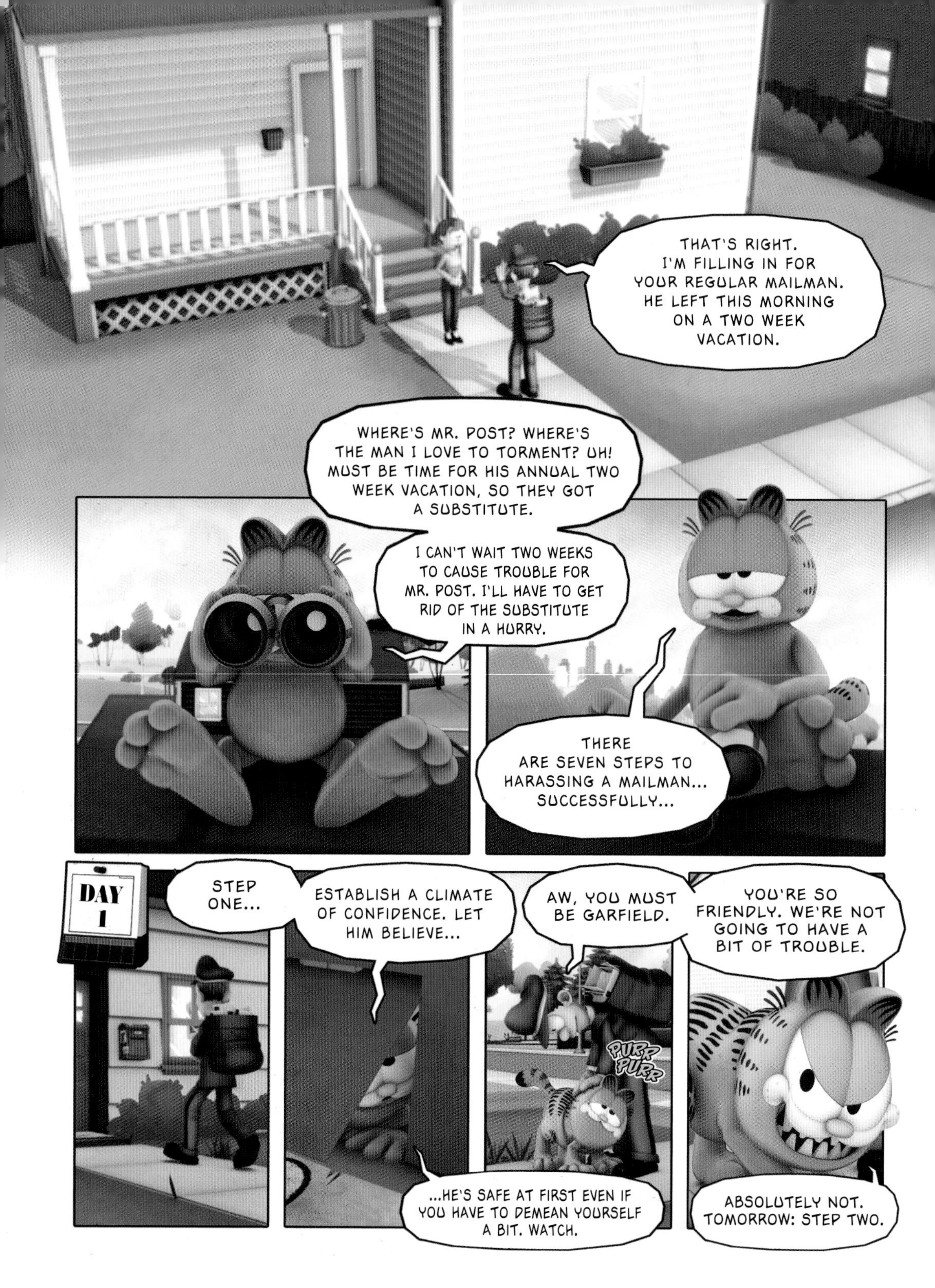
THAT'S RIGHT. I'M FILLING IN FOR YOUR REGULAR MAILMAN. HE LEFT THIS MORNING ON A TWO WEEK VACATION.
WHERE'S MR. POST? WHERE'S THE MAN I LOVE TO TORMENT? UH! MUST BE TIME FOR HIS ANNUAL TWO WEEK VACATION, SO THEY GOT A SUBSTITUTE.
I CAN'T WAIT TWO WEEKS TO CAUSE TROUBLE FOR MR. POST. I'LL HAVE TO GET RID OF THE SUBSTITUTE IN A HURRY.
THERE ARE SEVEN STEPS TO HARASSING A MAILMAN... SUCCESSFULLY...
DAY 1
STEP ONE...
ESTABLISH A CLIMATE OF CONFIDENCE. LET HIM BELIEVE...
...HE'S SAFE AT FIRST EVEN IF YOU HAVE TO DEMEAN YOURSELF A BIT. WATCH.
AW, YOU MUST BE GARFIELD.
PURR PURR
YOU'RE SO FRIENDLY. WE'RE NOT GOING TO HAVE A BIT OF TROUBLE.
ABSOLUTELY NOT. TOMORROW: STEP TWO.

39

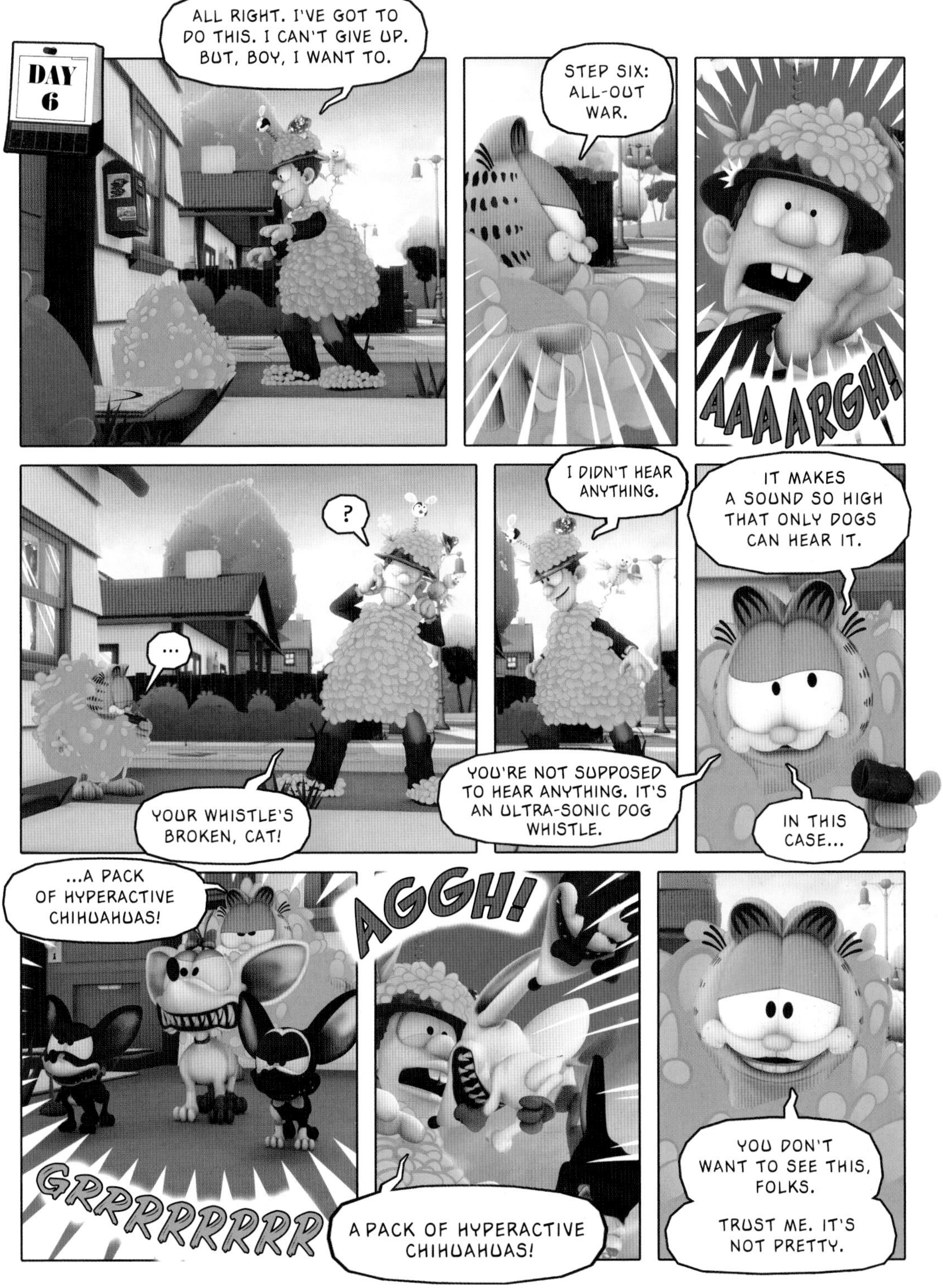
DAY 6
ALL RIGHT. I'VE GOT TO DO THIS. I CAN'T GIVE UP. BUT, BOY, I WANT TO.
STEP SIX: ALL-OUT WAR.
AAAARGH!
?
...
YOUR WHISTLE'S BROKEN, CAT!
I DIDN'T HEAR ANYTHING.
YOU'RE NOT SUPPOSED TO HEAR ANYTHING. IT'S AN ULTRA-SONIC DOG WHISTLE.
IT MAKES A SOUND SO HIGH THAT ONLY DOGS CAN HEAR IT.
IN THIS CASE...
...A PACK OF HYPERACTIVE CHIHUAHUAS!
GRRRRRRRRR
AGGH!
A PACK OF HYPERACTIVE CHIHUAHUAS!
YOU DON'T WANT TO SEE THIS, FOLKS.
TRUST ME. IT'S NOT PRETTY.

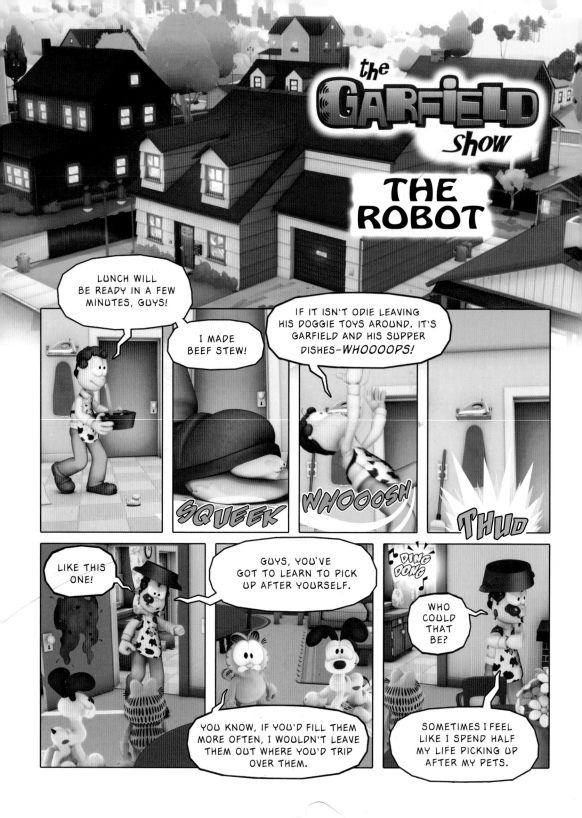

the GARFIELD show

THE ROBOT

LUNCH WILL BE READY IN A FEW MINUTES, GUYS!

I MADE BEEF STEW!

IF IT ISN'T ODIE LEAVING HIS DOGGIE TOYS AROUND. IT'S GARFIELD AND HIS SUPPER DISHES—*WHOOOOPS!*

SQUEEK

WHOOOSH

THUD

LIKE THIS ONE!

GUYS, YOU'VE GOT TO LEARN TO PICK UP AFTER YOURSELF.

YOU KNOW, IF YOU'D FILL THEM MORE OFTEN, I WOULDN'T LEAVE THEM OUT WHERE YOU'D TRIP OVER THEM.

DING DONG

WHO COULD THAT BE?

SOMETIMES I FEEL LIKE I SPEND HALF MY LIFE PICKING UP AFTER MY PETS.

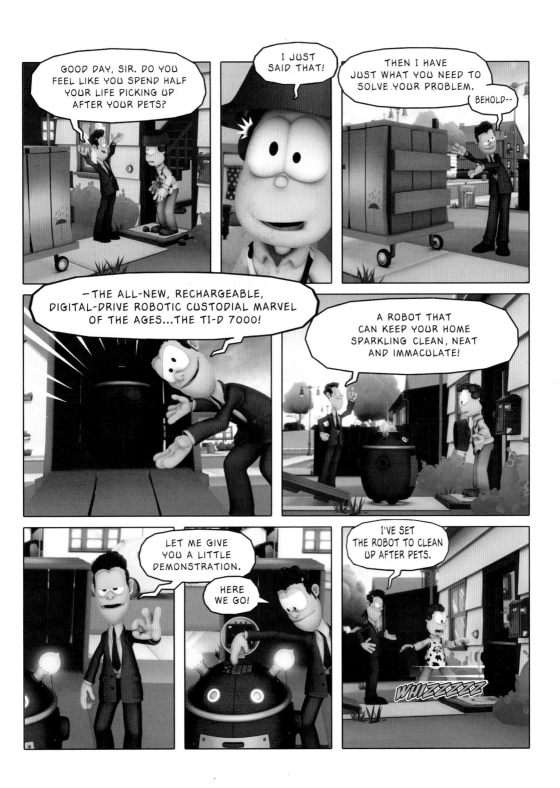

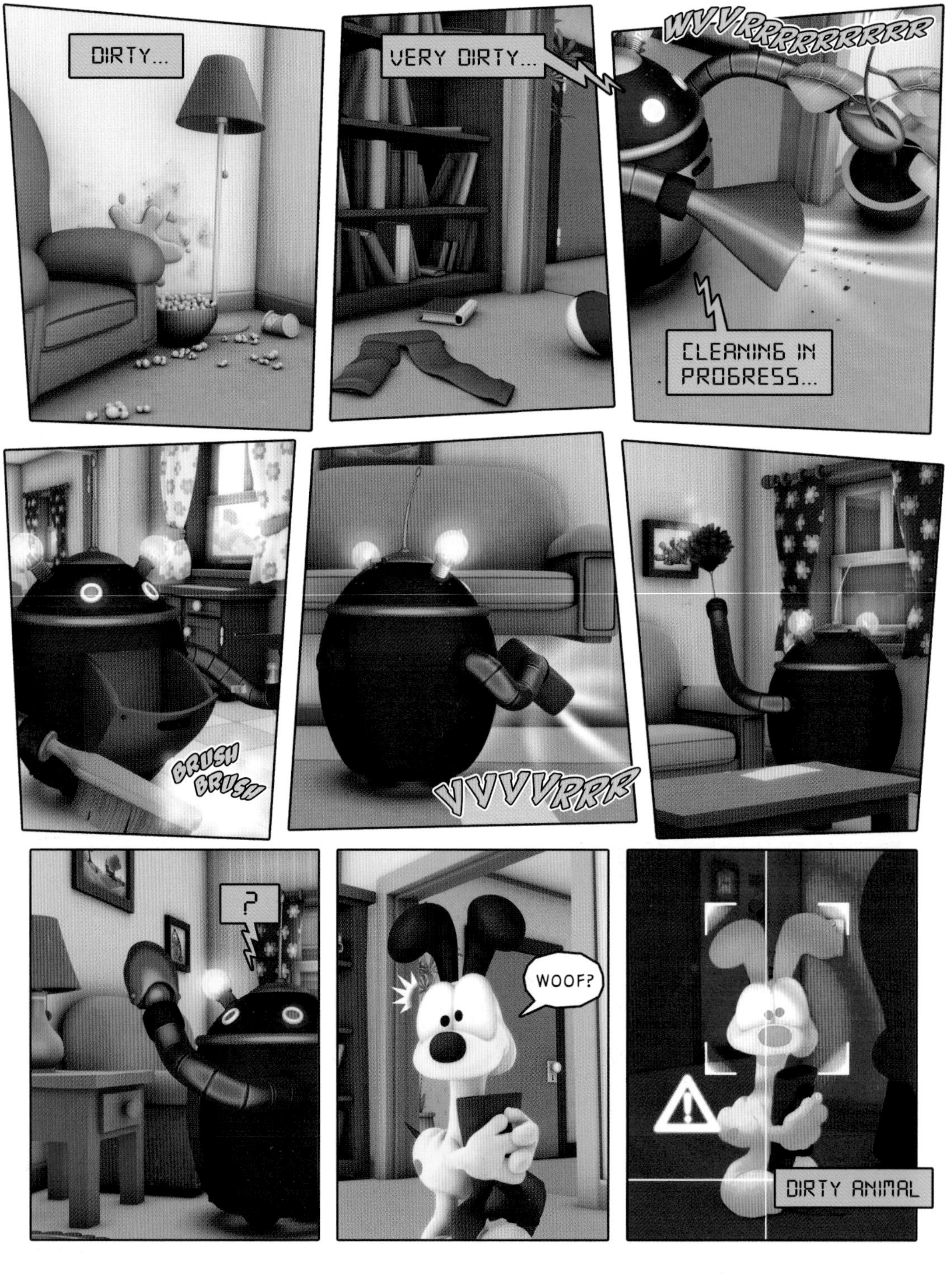
DIRTY...
VERY DIRTY...
WVVRRRRRRRRRR
CLEANING IN PROGRESS...
BRUSH BRUSH
VVVVRRR
?
WOOF?
DIRTY ANIMAL

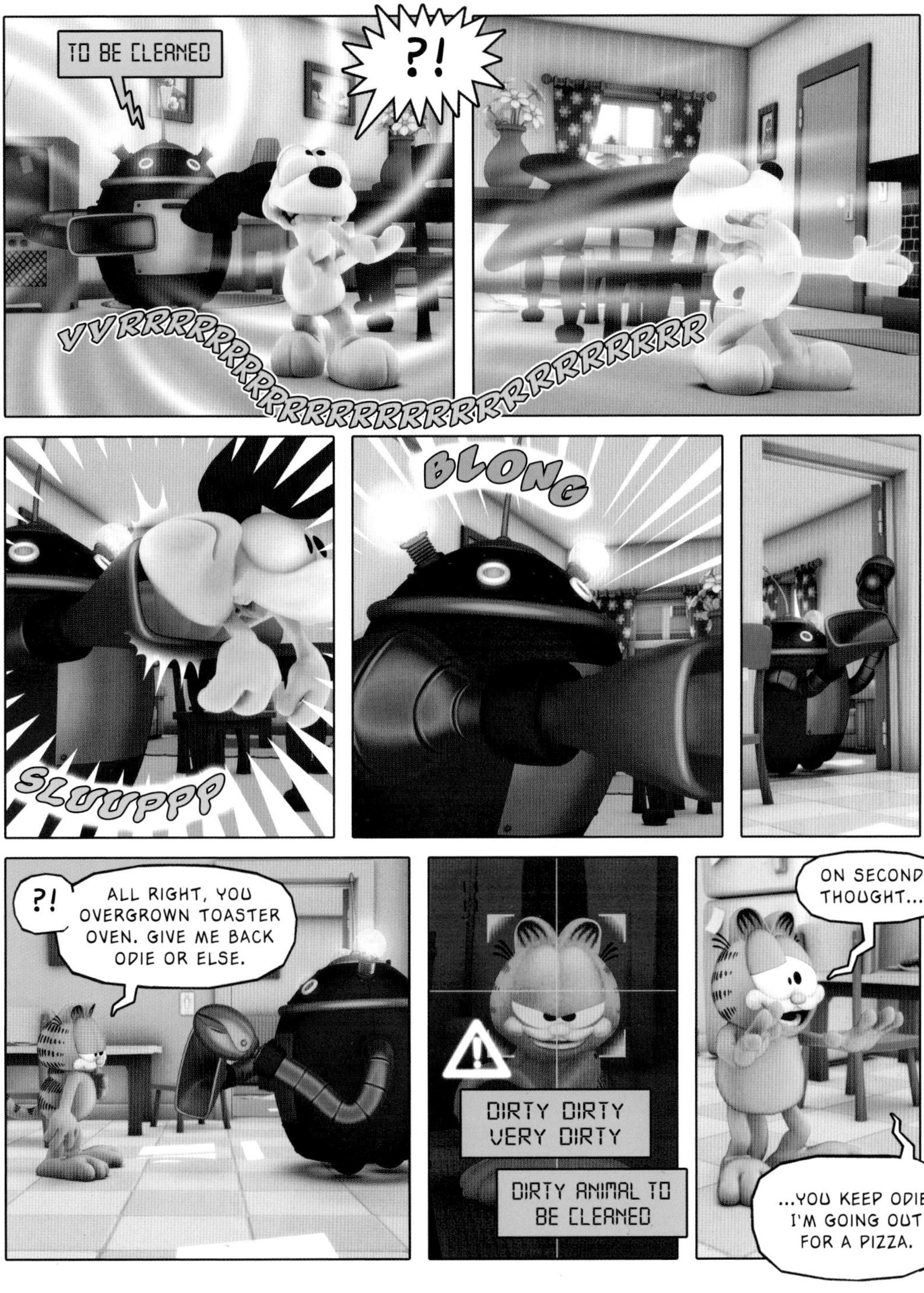
TO BE CLEANED
?!
VVRRRRRRRRRRRRRRRRRRRRRRRRRRR
SLUUPPP
BLONG
?!
ALL RIGHT, YOU OVERGROWN TOASTER OVEN. GIVE ME BACK ODIE OR ELSE.
DIRTY DIRTY VERY DIRTY
DIRTY ANIMAL TO BE CLEANED
ON SECOND THOUGHT...
...YOU KEEP ODIE. I'M GOING OUT FOR A PIZZA.

48

WATCH OUT FOR PAPERCUTZ™

Question: How are the Papercutz GARFIELD graphic novels physically like Garfield?
Answer: They both keep getting fatter!

Welcome to the fatter-than-ever first THE GARFIELD SHOW graphic novel from Papercutz, the cat-loving people dedicated to publishing great graphic novels for all ages. I'm your forever-dieting, lasagna-loving Editor-in-Chief, Jim Salicrup.

In case you think I'm just joking about our GARFIELD graphic novels getting fatter, just check out how many pages are in this graphic novel. I'll wait. Back so soon? Well, did you notice there's now twice as many pages in the new THE GARFIELD SHOW graphic novel as there were in any single GARFIELD & Co graphic novel? No need to thank me! In fact, if you're a true Garfield fan, I'm not the Jim you care about. That would be this guy:

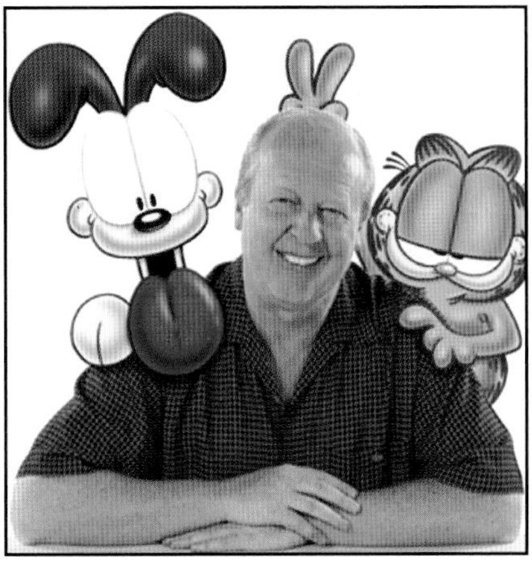

Jim Davis was born July 28, 1945 and was promptly dropped on his head, which would explain his life-long desire to sit around and draw silly pictures. His parents, Jim and Betty Davis, were farmers who raised Black Angus cows and feed crops for the cattle… not to mention 25 cats.

Jim and his little brother, Davey, grew up with a lot of responsibilities and chores, and lots of cats. When Jim was just a little boy he developed asthma — a breathing problem brought on by allergies (probably due to all the hay on the farm). Asthma makes you cough, hack, and wheeze, and Jim had to stay indoors a lot.

One day, when Jim's mom noticed he was bored, she shoved a pencil in his hand and gave him a stack of paper and told him to draw to "keep himself entertained." And he did. One of his first drawings was of a cow. Because it was hardly recognizable, Jim labeled it "cow." Next, he discovered that drawings were funnier if they had words. Before long, Jim had gotten pretty good at drawing. He couldn't stop! He drew on tables. He drew on walls. He even drew on the cattle!

Years later, Jim turned his attention to the comics pages and tried to figure out what was working and why. There were lots of dogs on the comics pages — Snoopy, Marmaduke, Belvedere — but no cats! Jim began sketching cats, drawing on his childhood memories of the 25 farm cats he grew up with. The cat that struck him as the funniest was a big fat grouchy character that he named Garfield after his opinionated grandfather, James Garfield Davis.

Papercutz is super-proud to be publishing THE GARFIELD SHOW, and I can't tell you excited I am that a certain fellow with the initials JD may be at the Papercutz booth at Comic-Con International: San Diego. Look for a complete report in THE GARFIELD SHOW #2 "Jon's Night Out." Until then, be sure to keep your lasagna in a safe place!

Thanks,

JIM

STAY IN TOUCH!

EMAIL:	SALICRUP@PAPERCUTZ.COM
WEB:	WWW.PAPERCUTZ.COM
TWITTER:	@PAPERCUTZGN
FACEBOOK:	PAPERCUTZGRAPHICNOVELS
BIRTHDAY CARDS:	PAPERCUTZ, 160 BROADWAY, SUITE 700, EAST WING, NEW YORK, NY 10038

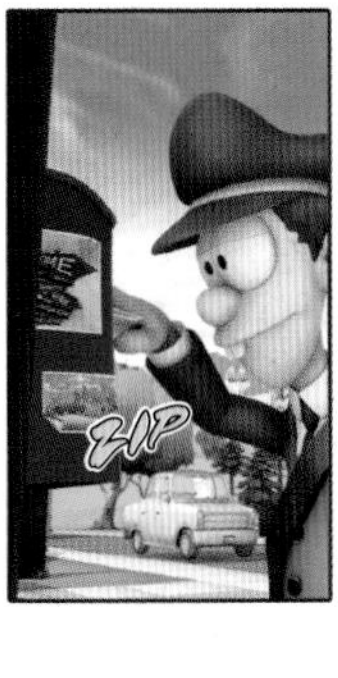
ZIP

THE END?

PAPERCUTZ™

WE KEEP TELLING YOU HOW MUCH WE LOVE CATS HERE AT PAPERCUTZ, SO WE THOUGHT WE'D RUN A FEW PICS OF OUR CATS AS PROOF POSITIVE!

HERE'S THE GARFIELD SHOW'S EDITOR MICHAEL PETRANEK'S CRIME-FIGHTING CAT, "ROBIN." TOGETHER, MICHAEL AND ROBIN ARE QUITE A DYNAMIC DUO!

WHILE PAPERCUTZ PRODUCTION COORDINATOR BETH SCORZATO CAN BOSS AROUND EVRYONE IN THE OFFICE, WE BET WHEN SHE GOES HOME, THE REAL BOSS IS HER CAT, "AKIMA."

HELPING HIM ON THE PRODUCTION OF OUR CLASSICS ILLUSTRATED GRAPHIC NOVELS ARE ORTHO'S CATS "LUNA" AND "CHLOE." OR DOES ORTHO ACTUALLY HELP THEM PUT IT ALL TOGETHER?

WHEN LOOKING FOR INSPIRATION ON HOW TO CREATE MORE ATTENTION FOR THE GARFIELD SHOW, PAPERCUTZ MARKETING DIRECTOR JESSE POST WILL OFTEN CONSULT HIS CATS "RUDIE" AND "JANGO."

PAPERCUTZ EDITOR-IN-CHIEF JIM SALICRUP GOT HIS CAT, "AZRAEL," AS A RESCUE. AZRAEL'S FORMER OWNER WAS REALLY A NASTY CHARACTER!

EDITOR MICHAEL PETRANEK'S FAMILY DOG, ZEUS, IS NOT A CAT AND DOES NOT BELONG HERE. BUT, HE KIND OF LOOKS LIKE ODIE, SO WE'LL LET THIS ONE SLIDE...

© Peyo - 2013 - Licensed through Lafig Belgium - www.smurf.com

More Great Graphic Novels from PAPERCUTZ™

DISNEY FAIRIES #12
"Tinker Bell and the Lost Treasure"
Tink must save Pixie Hollow in this story based on the hit DVD!

ERNEST & REBECCA #4
"The Land of Walking Stones"
A 6 ½ year old girl and her microbial buddy against the world!

DANCE CLASS #5
"To Russia, with Love"
The girls travel to Russia to perform "The Nutcracker"!

MONSTER #4
"Monster Turkey"
The almost normal adventures of an almost ordinary family... with a pet monster!

THE SMURFS #15
"The Smurflings"
Are the Smurfs getting... younger?

SYBIL THE BACKPACK FAIRY #4
"Princess Nina"
Sybil and Nina's excellent adventure through time!

Available at better booksellers everywhere!

Or order directly from us! DISNEY FAIRIES is available in paperback for $7.99, in hardcover for $11.99; ERNEST & REBECCA is $11.99 in hardcover only; DANCE CLASS is available in hardcover only for $11.99; MONSTER is available in hardcover only for $9.99; THE SMURFS are available in paperback for $5.99, in hardcover for $10.99; and SYBIL THE BACKPACK FAIRY is available in hardcover only for $11.99.

Please add $4.00 for postage and handling for the first book, add $1.00 for each additional book.

Please make check payable to NBM Publishing. Send to: PAPERCUTZ, 160 Broadway, Suite 700, East Wing, New York, NY 10038

(1-800-886-1223) or order online at papercutz.com